THE LAST OF THE LIGHT

THE LAST OF THE LIGHT

Alexander Shalom Joseph

The Last of the Light

ISBN: 978-1-949039-43-6
E-book ISBN: 978-1-949039-47-4

Orison Books
PO Box 8385
Asheville, NC 28814
www.orisonbooks.com

Cover photo by Alexander Shalom Joseph.

Manufactured in the U.S.A.

For my Grandma Joan.

I'm glad that within the beginnings and ends of so many lives and worlds, our little lights have overlapped for a time. Thanks for telling me your stories and the stories of our family stretching back across the sea. Now, here is one of mine, and like everything I do, it is yours and theirs too.

1

Any dew left from the hours of dark will soon turn to steam, rising like a spirit into the sky and disappearing into the dawn-softened air as the sun rises into full flame. The sound of a barking dog down the street steals a young man from sleep. He wakes and for a few groggy moments watches the light fall over his bed in shafts so solid they seem like something he could pluck out of the air.

This morning, a Tuesday in July in the hottest year in recorded history, is much like many others, full of climbing temperature, animal noises, and the fading traces of the daybreak pastels still smudging the edges of the sky. This morning is different too, though, for this is the young man's final chance to wake and gauge the shine of morning, his final chance to wake at all. These hours of heat are already moving quickly, but he supposes that every end comes too soon.

He crawls across his comforter, sits down at the desk in the corner of this, his childhood bedroom, opens a notebook, in which he has been keeping track of all that has happened in the last month: a ledger of waning hours, these little screams of time in a blur all leading to today. He flips to the beginning of the notebook and starts to read what he wrote just twenty-nine days before, a span which seems both a lifetime and no time from now, a whirling of days like dirty water in a drain, spiraling toward tonight.

29

I've decided to keep notes from today until the end.

I think I want to do this because of a story my mom told most nights before sleep when I was growing up. I remember the streetlights and the glow from our neighbors' houses filtering in, casting a soft light, like something gilded, spilling over my childhood bedroom. My sister and I on my twin bed and my mom in the chair at the desk in the corner of the room. Before the story, we were silent, in a half-darkness in which it quickly became hard to tell what was or wasn't a dream.

After the quiet, my mom would begin to speak. She told us the story of the Tzadikim Nistarim, the righteous ones, a group of thirty-six Jews from each generation tasked with justifying the existence of humanity to God. She'd explain how these people often don't know they're chosen and simply try to lead noble, humble lives. She went through her favorite examples of Tzadiks, as righteous ones are often called, throughout history: a story of a man who everybody thought was useless, but who could make it pour rain at his command; a young woman who took to the road wanting to be rid of people and their often evil ways, but who ended up bringing miracles wherever she went; and a grandmother who could make anything grow, even bringing crops back from brown and wilt with the guidance of her small, wrinkled, holy hands.

Each night my mom ended the story saying that we should live our lives like these members of our greater ancestry, as if we were made to be righteous, to be good, to make miracles unknowingly wherever we went, justifying to God above the world below. The last thing she said before she left the room, taking my sister with her and closing the door, was that maybe the goal isn't actually moving beyond this life or today, but living as a light sunk in the ever-reaching dark.

So here, in these weeks before what's to come, for the sake of sparking a pinprick of something bright in the deep, I'll do my best to detail for almighty eyes, in which I'm not sure I believe, my world and life and family. For what's the use of writing in times like these—in this end time—what's the use of writing at all, if not to do just this?

1

In the skinny light of just morning, in the dog sound and grass smell and yellow pollen wind, the young man sets down his notebook, puts on a pair of headphones, leans over, plugs them into his record player, and plays the album *For Emma Forever Ago*, then sits back in the chair and for a moment looks up at the seams of light tumbling in from the windows.

He loves this album because of how it sounds; it's one of his favorites because of its making, for doesn't the story of creation hold as much importance as the final result? While recording the album, Justin Vernon, was recovering from a sickness as well as the endings of many relationships at once. In a movement of mourning, Vernon retreated to a cabin in the middle of a dense New England wood with the splinters of his broken life, an acoustic guitar, and an antique recorder. There, the artist spent months living off thawed venison and cheap beer, working each day on what became the music the young man listens to now as he sits and watches the daylight grow stronger, as if an invisible hand is turning up a dial in the sky. For the past few minutes, he wanted the singer's falsetto set over muted minor chords to flow in the space between his ears and eyes forever.

But forever was a thing everybody lost a month ago and can never get back. The young man has been listening to this album more than ever in the last month, in the fringes of everything that ever was, hoping he can, as Vernon did, make something out of all this nothing he has, by means of the notebook on the desk before him. He picks up the notebook and begins to read from it again.

29

Yesterday, after a long day of work at the farm, I was sitting on the couch in the living room drinking a beer and leaning my head back, trying not to fall asleep, when my phone buzzed. I assumed it was a text from my girlfriend and checked it with the excitement that receiving a text from her, even after our years together, still makes me feel. It wasn't, however, a text but an alert, which I later learned had been sent to every cell phone, email, website, TV, and radio station on Earth.

In this message, the governments of every nation announced that the world would end in one month. The text assured that this wasn't a joke, that this was the true end of the world and would come as a result of an event which the world's best scientists had been unable to come up with a way of preventing. Thus, at the end of the month, the text continued, at around midnight (in the time zone in which I live and, I guess, am now destined to die) the end would occur. The text repeated that there was sadly no way to stop what was coming and gave an apology for any inconvenience this all may cause and an encouragement to be civil during this trying time.

The chaos of those small words on all our screens turned a quiet Wednesday night into something much louder: ablaze with fire, gunshots, sirens, and ringing phones.

Pretty much immediately, my roommates informed me they were going to the closest place with a beach, umbrella drinks, and babes, as they put it. Although I had a lot of questions about their plan, I kept my thoughts to myself as they enthusiastically punched holes in the drywall saying, "Fuck it, dude, we can do whatever we want. It's not like we have to worry about our deposits." Then, they piled into one of their Jeep Wranglers and drove off into a night lit by a quarter moon and riot fires that blotted out whatever stars there might have been. I stood waving and barefoot in the driveway of a house I'd wanted to myself for a long time, but I never expected it to take the end of the world for that to happen. I then called my girlfriend, she came over, we cried together until we were too tired to cry, then we went to bed, hoping to wake to a different world.

Instead, I woke before her to the same mess and decided that maybe, in the vein of the Tzadiks or the collective memory or even for my own sanity, I should try to get some words down on paper, to try to tell this story. I'm not sure why I chose to do this, perhaps as some sort of feral scream up to the sky, perhaps as a plea to a half-believed-in God to save us and to guide us in using this time, which now seems so important to use wisely, in some sort of meaningful way.

1

The dog down the street is making a noise now that is more than a bark, it is something piercing and awful and everywhere at once. The feeling in the sound, more than the sound itself, is what sticks in the young man's ears. He was hoping that today of all days he could sleep in and wake well-rested, but he woke up tired, two hours before breakfast time, which his mother had firmly set at eight thirty.

He supposes there is no escape from the end or from the dog either. The barking is so loud now he can barely think, even over the music coming through the headphones over his ears. He is listening to Townes Van Zandt's "(Quicksilver Daydreams of) Maria." He listened to this song over and over during the few days he was alone in his rental house, after his roommates were gone, after his girlfriend was gone. He sat on the couch in the living room where he first received the Announcement alert, playing this song on repeat, watching the passing time told in the shutters of light on the white-painted drywall. Those days on the couch, he thought of one lyric constantly, one in which Van Zandt details how the hands of the subject of the song sift the light, how it seems to surround this woman. The young man listens to his favorite lyric through his headphones now, and he thinks of his girlfriend, of the one who seems to shape the light around and inside of him, or used to, and how without her here all light seems much flatter and cold.

When he is reminded of her, things are sweet for a second, and then he is reminded further that she is gone and what was sweet is made more bitter than ever. The barking dog is bothersome because of the noise, but beyond the bother there is hurt, for the dog reminds him of her as well. His girlfriend wanted to get a dog, and he and she together spent a lot of time at the humane society looking for a future pet in rooms made of concrete and plexiglass. The dogs they passed had shiny wet noses and breath which fogged up the windows. There was something tragic about each of them, like a scar on their eye or a limp or a missing patch of fur. And yet, in spite of, or maybe because of their tragedies, these creatures were also cute.

His girlfriend invented a word to describe the adorable, miserable animals (and other such things) they saw, specifically in regard to one particular white pitbull mix with a red nose, spots on her feet, and a broken tail. This word was *tragicute.* The white pitbull had a plaster cast on her tail, and it was signed in multicolored markers by the staff of The Humane Society. The couple walked up to the pen and put their hands up to the glass, on the other side of which the wet pink nose pressed. The dog's tail began to wag, and the cast hit the wall on the edge of her pen. They could hear the quick and hollow sound of plaster on concrete. Eventually they began to move away, because they would not be able to buy a dog until at least September, when the two planned to move in together, a time now as unreal as everything else beyond this last night of the world. As they walked away, the sound of the tail and its plaster coating hitting the wall began to slow, until it stopped. His girlfriend then realized she had left her phone by the pen and went back toward it. As the dog heard them coming back, the wagging and the subsequent clacking started again. This sound of the plaster cast inspired his girlfriend to coin the *tragicute* term, and it was a term coined with tears in both of their eyes. This dog was something so sweet and shattered and soft and loving and lonely, and they left her there because they could not afford her and their leases didn't allow pets, and they walked past a hundred cages out into a day that seemed so much less bright than just an hour before.

Since the Announcement, there have been so many tragicute moments the young man wishes he could have pointed out to her, and he likes to imagine how she would laugh at these examples and how her nose would squinch up the way it always did when she laughed hard, but by now he has stopped thinking of tragic things as anything close to cute.

The tragedies of the everyday now have nothing about them which make him feel anything but dread.

And now the young man sits, alone in his childhood room, and listens to Van Zandt sing another song, "Waitin' 'Round to Die." The young man, too, is waiting around to die, and knows he can do nothing to change that, but he wishes that he could wait to die with her. But regardless of what the young man awaits or wishes or wants, she is gone and the song goes on and so does the day. He sighs, holding back a sob, and he looks back down at his notebook and flips to a page, the contents of which still burn like a sputtering match in his gut.

27

My girlfriend left yesterday. I woke alone and sat down here to write.

Her family's from back East, and she went that way as soon as she could. It broke my heart to see her go, although I would've done the same thing if our places were reversed. She got on a converted school bus labeled "Gov" in drippy black paint on the front and both sides, provided to take people across the country. While we were waiting in the line for the bus, still not fully believing any of what was going on was real, she asked me to come with her. She told me how, the night before, she'd asked her parents if I could come and be with them and they'd said yes, but I couldn't go. She knew I had my own family to be with, but she couldn't leave without having asked me to come on the chance I somehow said yes.

But I said no, and the word fell out into the open air like a ball of metal from my mouth, sinking, making everything heavy and dark.

Pressed together in our final moments as an *us* before we again became just a *me* and a *her*—or each of us just an *I*—we stood outside the idling bus, drowning in the murmur of loss and panic, sweating in humidity so thick that you could almost wet your hand by dragging it across the air, although neither of our hands were free and we were holding each other as tight as we could for the last time. The sun was beating down so brightly it washed everything out into white molten blurs and the stink of the buses and the buzzing of the worried crowd made the brightness and the wetness and the temperature weigh down on our bodies, seemingly growing heavier the closer we got to the doors of the bus.

On her back was a backpack we bought for a trip to Europe we'd planned to take this fall but which now only exists in the hopes we had of how it would be to see the world together, and even those seem dull and somehow far away. The backpack was full of her favorite clothes and some snacks for the ride, which I helped her pack. She was wearing blue jeans and my grey sweatshirt, and her hair was in a loose ponytail at the back of her head. I figured then if she was wearing something of mine, at least I could kind of feel like I was there providing some sort of warmth or protection to her, although this thought didn't provide much solace at all.

I was wearing a pair of broken flip flops held together with electrical tape, a t-shirt she got for me for Hanukkah last year with "I Love Jew Very Much" printed on the back, and some blue shorts I've had since my high school gym class—my name written in long-faded marker on the front left leg in a white box. The outfits may seem irrelevant or useless to describe, but they're burned into my mind, every detail of that afternoon seems to be, the way every moment since the Announcement seems like it's happened in technicolor, the way time stays with you when you try to hold it back, like it stains you, like all the worst moments are vivid and stuck somewhere inside.

We held hands in the line, and the air reeked like diesel and the pungent cloy of body odor lined with fear. The gaggle of crying and blank faces moved onto the bus, and we inched forward with it until she was standing on the brown rubber steps. She looked down at me, seeming to want to say something but we both realized that no sentence could change what was going on. No words were strong enough to carry all the weight we held in our throats, so we said nothing.

When people behind us impatiently asked if I was getting on, she leaned down and kissed me and then nodded for me to back up. I did, and as I moved back it seemed the very ground beneath my feet was sinking and I was falling into nothing. She moved to a seat by a window at the middle of the bus and waved at me. She was crying. So was I.

The bus started to move. I started to move with it, planning to run beside it until my feet or my flip flops or my heart gave out, but one of the soldiers helping keep everybody civil and in line held me back. I stood in the dirt, crying and sweating and reaching for her as the bus blended with the line of other buses that kicked up dust which swirled and met with the sun, blurring the lines between sky and ground. Everything was formless and empty. I stood in the superheated haze, dry throated. The buses faded to specks on the red-smeared horizon, and then the soldier told me to move along.

There was always more time for us, until there wasn't.

Much later, after stumbling home, I fell asleep, hoping that when I woke everything would've been a bad dream.

Instead, I came to in throbbing dark in the middle of the hot night in my dusty clothes, overheated and alone.

1

The young man's rental house was thirty minutes from his parents' house by car and five minutes on foot from where his girlfriend used to live. Within three days of his roommates' departure, two days after his girlfriend's departure, and after many hours staring at the walls in shock from all the loss and change—not to mention one of the houses next door being set on fire—after all that, somebody threw a brick through the front window of the young man's house. There was nothing to do then but be grateful for the fact that his father was a survivalist nut. Minutes after the brick made shatter and shard of the front window of his home, in the last ever hour of cell phone service, the young man, crying, called his father and asked to be saved from this mess. Thirty minutes after they got off the phone, his father pulled up in his lifted, semi-armored truck, lowered the window, and asked his son if he needed a ride. The young man was never happier to hear one of his father's stupid one-liners.

His first notebook entry after telling of the departure of his girlfriend comes after many days of not writing at all, days spent feeling as though there was nothing worth trying to justify, no use in writing to an empty expanse of black above and within, no use in anything really.

22

Today, my mom decided we needed to get some sort of schedule together because, well, we were a mess.

We had to learn we needed structure the hard way. These past three days since I got home, things have not been healthy. I spent three days in a row drunk on whatever cheap beer I could find in the garage, slurring my words, blubbering on the couch in the living room, feeling the full crush of the end, staring at the day reflected on the walls, wondering if it was worth it to live through this final month. Meanwhile, my mom and dad stayed in their room, emerging every so often in their underwear to get water or a new jar of pickles or to smoke cigarettes on the patio outside, but not really saying anything to anybody. I have no idea where my grandpa—who we call Zayde, which means grandfather in Yiddish—was during those days. As far as I know, he might've hopped the high and electrified fence in the front yard and wandered the street.

On those first days, the house echoed with pillow-muffled wails, angry groans, faint folk music behind doors, the crunching of empty beer cans, and, coming in from the distance beyond the windows, the sounds of gunshots, fireworks, and the dog down the street. I'm pretty sure none of us ate a real meal during that time: we were too full of misery.

But today, on my fourth morning here, my mom called a family meeting. We gathered in the living room. The light through the windows was painful and white. Before the start of the meeting, I'd been passed out on the couch, having drunk myself into a shallow and restless immobility the night before. My mom woke me up by banging a saucepan with a wooden spoon right next to my head.

During the meeting, I wore a blanket over my head and squinted, clutching my stomach, trying to force some oatmeal down my throat to quell the nausea. Zayde stood by the front window, eating almonds he pulled from the pockets of his cardigan and loudly sipping grape soda even though it was nine in the morning. My dad sat on the couch beside me. He had an unlit cigarette in his mouth and no shirt on. His old man muscles, sun-faded tattoos, and salt-and-pepper chest hair moved as he breathed. I could smell the cigarette even though it was unlit and it wasn't helping my nausea at all.

My mom stood in front of us gesturing in ways she inherited from her father. While she talked, she held the spoon she'd used to bang on the saucepot to wake me up, emphasizing her points by moving it like a baton, acting as conductor of the rest of our lives. She said we needed to create some sort of system where things could be normal or at least kind of normal, because *this* wasn't working. When she said *this* she gestured with the wooden spoon toward the beer cans and crumpled blankets scattered around the floor of the living room. I groaned. My dad flicked the unlit cigarette up and down with his lips. Zayde softly burped. Outside, something far away exploded. The dog down the street barked shrilly toward a silent sky.

My mom said she loved us all too much to watch us waste our final days, that so many people were out there going through God knows what, and that we were lucky enough to be together as a family, or at least most of a family. We were lucky enough to have a safe place with enough food and water and so on to get us through the end in relative comfort.

When she said *and so on*, she gestured to my dad with the spoon, who shrugged, looking like a puppy caught in the garbage. She concluded her speech, of course, with the story of the Tzadiks, how the family should be living examples of good humanity to God, how we can be righteous—but she stopped mid-sentence, saying she wasn't going to bore us with religious talk, but, for her sake, it would be great if we could create some schedule in order to make our time together worthwhile and not any more depressing than it already was. My dad said he "agreed with mama" and then took the cigarette out of his mouth, motioned to Zayde with it, and they both went outside. I went to my bedroom to try to transcribe the last few days into my journal and my mom said she had an idea for a short story about a young woman who gets hit by a car and ends up having a conversation with a God who looks just like her father before being resuscitated at a hospital.

Sitting here now, still hungover from the last few days of drinking, and sore from sleeping on the couch, I can't believe that the world has come to this, that of all things to write about in a life, instead of love or some adventure, I'm writing about my family facing annihilation. This isn't the sort of book I ever hoped to write. Hell, I don't even know if I ever hoped to write any book, but since it's the one I am writing—after everything, after the end of the whole world—I might as well do it properly. And to do that I figure I should put to paper these people with whom I'll be spending my last days on Earth and who've made me who I am.

To start let me talk a little bit about where I am and build out from there into everything else. I'm in my childhood bedroom. This room is in the back corner of the house, next to the bathroom. In this room, there is a twin bed and a small desk where I write this now, sitting on a stiff chair where my mom used to sit when I was growing up and tell me and my sister the stories of the Tzadiks. I brought with me some clothes, this notebook, a collection of my favorite records, and my record player. The music on my phone no longer works, and I knew that my parents would have power on account of my dad's generators, so the records were a must.

In this room, there are two windows. One of these windows looks at the back yard fence and into the neighbor's yard, which shows nothing but dead grass. The other gives a view of a stretching sky, gridded with telephone wire and branches, which move like reaching hands in the wind. Although I'm not sure if anybody in this neighborhood is even still alive, it's clear somebody's dog certainly is, for it woke me up this morning and has bothered me with barking ever since. I want to go look for the dog, to bring it home and have it with us for the end, but my family forbade me going out into the street, saying it was just too unsafe to leave.

Since I moved out of my parents' place around nine years ago, my mom and dad have used this room for storage. There are stacks of my mom's books—almost up to the ceiling—in every corner of the room: books on Marxism, literary theory and criticism, and anthologies of poetry. My mom is a creative writing and Jewish studies professor at the local university, or at least she was, when people still had lives outside of their homes. She is also the author of many books that blend Jewish history with sci-fi and horror elements, her most famous being *Shtetl 51*, which is about an alien invasion in a 19th-century Belarusian Jewish shtetl, a setting based on the town where her ancestors were born. She had so many books when I was growing up, I remember there being at least one big stack or full bookshelf in every room. Coming home for dinner and visits since I moved out, I often wondered where all the books had gone. When I moved back in I found out.

But I guess I really should've started by introducing Zayde, because without him none of us would be here. He landed at Ellis Island at the age of eight, with his brothers and his mother by his side, a grey cardboard suitcase in his hand, shaken by his proximity to the ongoing war against our people from which he narrowly escaped. The first thing he did upon arrival in this wide and callous country was switch his yarmulke for a paper-boy cap, which he hasn't taken off since. For nearly seventy years, he worked manufacturing clothes in a crowded building: drawing, designing, and sewing custom suits and dresses with knowledge gleaned in his hometown, known then for its textiles and known now for massacres, barbed wire, and mass graves. My mom is his only child. She came to this area for her master's degree and met my dad, who grew up on a farm about three hours from here. At a hospital about eight minutes away, my sister and I were born, first her and then me three years and six months later. We were raised in this house where we all now—except for my sister—wait to die.

Eventually, after working seven days a week since the day he immigrated, Zayde was forced into retirement. In his early eighties, he began to forget things. After having spent over seventy years of his life speaking and working in English in New York, and with a diagnosis of dementia, he slowly began to forget the language of this country and started to only be able to think and speak and make sense of the world through Yiddish, the mame loshn, or mother tongue, which, despite who knows how many languages he used in his hometown, was the one that remained in his head after everything else had left. After Grandma, who we call Bubbe, died, he was left in an apartment alone, slowly losing the ability to read the words around him or speak to anybody but the other old Jewish immigrants in his apartment building, so my mom flew to New York and brought him back here. She will sometimes refer to this trip as the second great migration, the act of leaving that city and ending up beneath these wide skies.

We put Zayde in an old age home close by, where he communicated with the nurses in points and gestures and where they communicated back to him in the same. We would've had him live with one of us, but the doctors and nurses told my parents it was best to have him in a place where he could be under professional care at all times. After the Announcement, of course, there was no choice but to bring him home.

Mom and I used to visit him on Friday nights and bring him his favorite meal, a pastrami on rye with pickle-flavored chips on the side. This was the closest thing we had to a Shabbat, as we have always been more culturally Jewish than religiously observant. Zayde fled Europe to find solace and safety on these shores, and that is more or less what he found. And there, at the old age home, three generations ate our semi-holy meal under fluorescent lights thick with the smell of disinfectant and cafeteria food. We sat together in plastic cushioned chairs, my mom translating what Zayde had to say. Although there is not much of what he says that I can understand, Zayde has yet to forget these three English phrases: *Jesus Christ*, *atta boy*, and *nope*. These need no translation.

After the Announcement, one of the first panicked calls my mom received, besides my own, was from the nursing home saying someone needed to come pick up Zayde or he'd be left to starve in a lightless building on the north side of town. Apparently, the nurse who called felt he deserved better than to die surrounded by those who'd been left behind. When my mom went to pick him up, the nurse told her not to forget to buy a case or two of a specific local grape soda that he'd become addicted to after they installed a vending machine at the home. "And thus," as my mom tells it in her overdramatic way, "on the way home through the fire and brimstone," while Zayde waited in the car, she ran inside the grocery store, left some money on the unattended cash register, and grabbed a cart full of the grape soda. If it counts, this is the last purchase made by anybody I know.

1

The young man glances up from the notebook, thinking he is glad his grandfather is here with them at the end, staying in the guest room down the hall. Sometimes at night when his grandfather thinks everybody has gone to sleep, from under the guest room door the young man can see the honey light of a desk lamp, smell cigarettes that the grandfather must have stolen from the young man's father, and hear the sound of jazz records brought here in a cardboard box from the home. Although the young man mourns the distance that age and language and memory have created between him and his oldest living ancestor, hearing his grandfather's music makes the young man feel like he is not so far away from him after all.

Along with the fast piano and squealing brass, the young man can often hear, muffled by the plaster and stained wood and white paint, seeping out along with sweet light, the sound of an old man dancing the darkness away in broken heeled slippers and grey wool socks. And in that movement, done for no reason other than the joy of it, the young man can see the essence of a Tzadik in his grandfather, the small righteousness of being a holy fool alone and dancing in the night, justifying the world to God with the joy of these small movements. The young man now stands up and opens the window to let in the day, a day gorgeous and alive with peeping birds and the heavy humid swelter of the July air.

Happy with the way he described his grandfather, feeling like he did him justice—even a divine sort of justice—he turns the page to read how he described the rest of his family.

21

If I'm going to introduce my parents here, I should do it in the way they always introduce themselves, which is with the story of how they met. I've heard the story of my parents' meeting more than anything else, other than maybe the story of the Tzadiks.

The story goes that Mom was working her first teaching job at a community college where a company at which Dad was a day laborer and carpenter had been hired to help build a new science and technology wing. This was before my dad started his own company and before my mom was tenured, way before us children were born, back when there was nothing in the future but hope and fantasies of flying cars.

My dad usually starts the story, accented by his slight southern drawl and his seeming inability to pronounce the letter *g* in any word ending with *ing*. Mom usually interrupts, filling in for what she calls "narrative clarity." As Dad tells it, they met one day when he was "mindin' my own business, cuttin' some two-by-fours for a wall I was framin', and while I was cuttin', I was sweatin' somethin' fierce with a carpenter's pencil tucked behind my ear and an American Spirit in my mouth." Then, he continues, "this pretty little lady walks past, carryin' a whole bunch-a books, her hair a holy mess." He was so distracted, he "done gone and cut my finger off with the table saw blade." There was a huge spurt of blood, apparently, and this is where my mom usually butts in: "It was a comically large spray of blood," she will say, "which jetted across the ceiling and made a sound loud enough to cause me to drop my books and run" toward the man who would eventually become my dad.

I have to say here that the dropping of the books for anybody else is dramatic, but for my mom, it's even more so, as she raised her children with the belief that books are sacred objects and that we should move each page as carefully as possible. Her dropping books must have meant she was really startled, that something particularly important was going on.

The story continues with my mom running toward my dad to see if he is okay, but my dad is already running toward her, as he says, "like a chicken with its head cut off." They collide and end up on the floor, covered in his blood and her school papers. "Pages of half-graded essays, blood droplets, sawdust, and love filled the air around us," is another thing my mom always says. She usually continues, saying something about time standing still as their eyes met, at least until they realized they had to take him to the hospital to get his finger stitched back on.

My dad usually goes on to say how the folks at the hospital thought he was "havin' a heart attack or somethin', 'cause my heart was beatin' so fast, but it was only 'cause I'd fallen in love," which I always find hard to believe but let him say because I guess I think it's sweet. My dad usually ends the story by saying "them stitches didn't hurt 'cause the glowin' of my heart was takin' up every ounce of feelin' in my body."

1

And here, the young man pauses at his recollection of the story of the two people who would eventually make and raise him, of their enduring love—and for a minute, this love fills him up with a feeling not unlike the light shining into his room. He has always been a bit of a romantic, and the drama of the story of his parents' meeting has always tickled that part of him that buzzes at love. But this time, the warmth fades to a cold lack, like being caught without a jacket on a day with an extreme temperature drop, as he remembers his own love story and how it ended so abruptly in the harsh sun and dust. He shakes his head side to side for a second, trying to push away this creeping feeling, and starts to read again, not wanting to sink into the thoughts of her, of all that has happened. Can he let himself think of her on this last day without losing it? Without sinking into that feeling of falling forever that haunted him after she left? He turns another page of the notebook and starts to read in order to distract himself.

21

Along with being a laborer who goes around falling in love with big-haired women and cutting parts of himself off, my dad has been planning for the end of the world for as long as anybody can remember. In his words, he has always known that at some point "shit was goin' to hit the fan." He started prepping for the end when he was a "youngin'," collecting candy bars and canteens of water under his bed, saving money in his socks, and preparing different sites of storage and go-bags around every house he ever lived in. Here, at this house, he has several backup generators, a deep well, rainwater collection tanks, solar power, and enough food to last us years. But the end we are facing isn't a zombie apocalypse, civil war, nuclear war, alien invasion, apocalyptic virus, or anything else of the sort. No, we're facing annihilation, and all the prepping in the world can't save the world itself.

The solar power and the generator provide enough electricity for us to watch movies and run the record players, oven, and water heater, while the well and rainwater tanks provide us with water for baths and hydration. Even though I hated having to inventory cans of tuna and do other sorts of survivalist chores on the weekends when I was growing up, especially while my friends got to go on picnics or hikes or do anything else besides helping my dad with his "preppin'," I guess I'm glad he did what he did, so that we can live out this end in relative comfort.

And it would be dishonest somehow, maybe even a disservice, to not talk about all that my dad has, let's say, collected. Included in his stockpile are dozens of cases of beer, thousands of rolls of toilet paper, hundreds of jars of instant coffee, home-canned vegetables from the farm where I used to work, store-bought cans of soup and beans, what must be close to a literal ton of packaged oatmeal, two large chest freezers of different cuts of elk meat, and about thirty pints of different flavors of ice cream (some of which we keep in the house for easier access).

Along with all that, the stockpile includes a lot of pickles. There used to be a tire place in town where my dad bought a jar of pickles every year as he waited to get studded snow tires put onto his various trucks. Each year my dad talked on and on about the pickles, how there was nothing else like them, and each year we all rolled our eyes in unison.

One year, while getting his tires changed, my dad heard that the pickle company, owned by the wife of the mechanic, was not doing so well. So, as my dad tells it, he "got to talkin' and decided to help them folks out of their pickle-pickle" and ended up purchasing their whole stock. The result was about two thousand jars of pickles, which are stacked in the garage between the toilet paper and the canned goods. Thus, one of the defining tastes of the past month has been pickles, as we've been eating at least one jar per day, if not way more than that. One of the worst, but also most entertaining, parts of the pickle situation is that when we finish a jar, Zayde usually drinks the juice. While we've been running out of different kinds of food over the last month, we might've needed a lifetime to finish the pickles.

But pickles aren't the most bizarre thing my dad hoarded. My least favorite, and of course my dad's most prized part of the stockpile, the most embarrassing stop on the required tour of the house, which every girlfriend and friend I've brought home has been subjected to, is located in a closet my dad built in the back corner of the garage, behind a creaking door, illuminated by a drawstring bulb for the most dramatic reveal possible. Stacked from the concrete floor to the foil-covered insulation on the garage ceiling is what's got to be at least four thousand boxes of turquoise, full-bodied American Spirit cigarettes.

Many ask why, to which I shrug, and my dad answers the same way every time: "If the world's gonna end, I'm gonna have myself a smoke or two, before I myself get smoked."

Since he's my dad, I of course have my biases and triggers around him, the stockpile and the bad jokes, but despite everything, I sort of pity him. Sure, we have a lot of packages of maple oatmeal, cuts of elk, jars of pickles, and thousands of cigarettes, but no amount of prepping, no meat nor pickles nor hands pressed in prayer—nor my writing to make sense of all this, to call upon God and show him that maybe all this is worth saving—none of this, nothing, can stop what's coming at the end of this month.

1

The young man pauses after reading the last few lines of his journal, at the mention of his writing as some call to God. He thinks for a while about what that means to him. While his mother has spent her life studying Jewish history, she did not raise her children in the religion. They rarely went to temple, but they did light the menorah and give gifts at Hanukkah, a holiday which they celebrated in part because it coincided with the Christmas break she had from school. The family ate apples dipped in honey on Rosh Hashanah and spoke of what they wanted to bring into their new year; they fasted as best they could on Yom Kippur and tried to hold in their minds and hearts what they had lost. On Passover they ate matzah and horseradish and parsley and drank four glasses of wine and celebrated the freedom of a people whom they still carried in their bones. But they rarely spoke of God.

And so most of what the young man knows about his culture and the faith is from offhand stories, secularized traditions, folktales, and whispered ideas of where he came from, what the people there were like, and what they lived their lives for. With all this as the basis for his connection to the religion of a people he knows he is a part of, but which he is not sure how much a part, the young man is not sure, either, if he believes in God. And not having been forced to believe as a child, he has had to come to understand what this weighty word means to him on his own.

If somebody were to have asked him a month ago what he thought about the subject, he may have said something about God being there in little ephemeral moments, in the passing V's of geese in the sky, in the sight of a sprout poking out of the earth, in the heat between the bodies of him and his girlfriend as they slept beside each other in the night. If somebody were to have asked him a month ago, he may have said God was a gentle hand on the back of everybody, providing loving encouragement and a push in the right direction. But now if he were asked about God, there would be no mention of a presence, just a lack, and how that lack rings louder than any presence ever could, how that lack is going to shatter the world.

1

In part because he needs to but in part to stop thinking of God and tonight and everything else, the young man leaves his room and walks to the bathroom down the hall.

Looking in the mirror, water dripping from the edges of his face, the sweet sting of mint in his mouth, he realizes he will never get older than he is today. This month, he has spent more time than ever looking at his own face, knowing what he sees will be what he looks like when he dies.

At the beginning of this month, he would worry the weight of the coming end would eventually crush him, that the collective pain of everybody he loves would become too much. He feared a great falling would come over him and that he would simply cease to exist, smothered by billions of pounds of all that ever was. There was so much to hold, so much suffering behind everyone's eyes, and in his own too—so much ash from the burned up future, fluttering like white hot petals in the wind. Yet, somehow, he remained; he stayed alive, here to look at himself amidst the dried dots of toothpaste and water on the mirror in the glossy, greyed light of the bathroom. Somehow he remained.

Freshened up, but not quite ready to face the family and make real his last ever breakfast, which will be served in half an hour, he retreats back to his room to read.

20

Let me describe my parents, what they look like, who they are, give you a taste of them—although who is this *you* I'm writing to? There will soon be nobody left to do anything, most certainly nobody left to read these scribbles in a pink notebook with a unicorn pooping a rainbow on the front, which I got at a yard sale for ten cents last summer. But I guess there has to be a you, because there is somebody I'm writing to, maybe God, maybe all the Tzadiks, their spirits, maybe just a different version of myself. Whoever you are, I think you should know who they are, these people I love, and what we did, before we're all gone.

My mom's less than five feet tall and has already read ten books in the time we've been confined to this house. She wears very thick, wide-rimmed glasses, like the ones popular in the eighties. Her hair's so curly it extends about a foot in every direction around her head like a dirty-blonde halo. Another one of her defining traits is that she's crazy about my dad, but for the life of me, I've never been able to understand what my parents have in common, other than that they fell in love at first sight. They both say their love is a mystery, but it's the best mystery they've ever found themselves a part of.

When I asked my mom what she loved most about my dad, she thought in the way she always does, chewing on the back of a pen cap and twirling a ringlet of her hair while her eyes seemed far away. After some time, she looked directly at me and said the thing she loved most about her husband was his mind.

This answer surprised me and my dad. In fact, he let out a little hoot when she said it, all of us sitting on the patio after dinner as the sun stained the sky like a spilled set of paints. Hell, I think it surprised her, but she said it with confidence nonetheless. She explained, when asked why, that what she loves about her husband's mind, and thus her husband himself, is how present he is, how curious, how comical, how in the moment and off-the-cuff he is, how himself he is.

She went on to explain that my dad once introduced her to a song called "Peng! 33" by Iron and Wine. In it the singer describes how there are things more powerful than fear, such as curiosity, and that this curiosity can be both simple and profound at once. Through these lyrics she found some insight into this man she'd fallen so deeply in love with many years before. She was able to understand that my dad's prepping didn't come only from fear of the end but also from curiosity about survival, a deep interest in seeing how things would end up. My mom explained how she came to understand my dad as simple yet also as prodigious, as a lyric in the song says, prodigious meaning something remarkably great, something extremely wide and edgeless. And that's how she's always felt with him, an endlessness, a profound simplicity, an ease in knowing that together they will face whatever will come with a smile and some dumb jokes, that there will always be more curiosity than fear. "That is why I love him," she said, "along with so many other things. The way the gold teeth in his smile glint in the sun. The way he smokes his cigarettes like Kurt Cobain. The way time slows when I'm in his arms."

I then asked the same question to my dad. He slicked his hair back with his hand, took a half-empty pack of American Spirits out of his shirt pocket, tapped a cigarette up and took it out with his mouth. He lit it with a quick flip-and-flick of his zippo, then sat back on the patio chair, looking up at the violet sky, and breathed in deep, letting the smoke out through his nose, his eyes closed.

After a few more puffs, he said he used to think he could figure everybody out. "See," he said, "I was raised breakin' broncos with my daddy, who died long before any of his grandchildren could be born, before he could even meet his daughter-in-law. And you might think that breakin' broncos is about seein' the wild retreat in their eyes or hurtin' them until they're tame, but I learned early, when I was just a teen in too-blue jeans, my first cigarettes at my lips, that the real work is creatin' some sort of bond with the beast. I learned that the way to tame anythin' is to make it your own, to let the thing own you too, the way to make this work, the pact between beatin' hearts is allowin' the body of the beast to move in the same way as yours. And in order to do that," he said, "you gotta to listen real close, notice the little twitches, smells, and sounds that make somethin' what it truly is." Having been raised like this, when he went out in the world, my dad explained, he turned his sensitive eye onto everybody he saw, and within a few minutes he was able to understand most people.

By my dad's stoic standard, this was a lot of speech at once. The way he was talking about growing up, the way he was sort of waxing philosophical, was a side of him I'd never really seen before, and in this side I could see some of what my mom was saying, that sort of edgelessness, like there was so much to him that I'd never understood and I guess never will. He'd never talked like this before around me, and I realized that I'd never get to know my parents, or really anybody else, fully. Maybe I never would've anyway, but now I certainly won't.

My dad went on to say, "My daddy took me out of school after eighth grade to help on the farm, help with the broncos and the dirt," and he continued describing that despite his lack of schooling, there's a clearness in his head that most don't have, a thereness that isn't easy to find, a way he can see straight into people, figure them out quickly. "But this woman, the one of my dreams and my wakin' life too, she is the only one I ain't never been able to fully figure out" my dad concluded. With her, his bronco eyes could never pin down the full story, never cut to the core. She surprises him every day with that whip of a mind she has. Taking another drag of his cigarette, he said, "That's why I love her, because she is truly one of a kind, along with the fact that she just glows up a room when she walks in, if she wants to, and that seein' her, even after all this time and two kids, makes me feel like there's somethin' with wings in my gut."

1

The young man smiles as he reads this last passage, having put on the album *Around the Well* by Iron and Wine, an album his dad showed him a long time ago but which means more now that he knows his mom loves it too. He skips to the song "Peng! 33," which his mother mentioned in the passage he wrote weeks before. As he recalls it, that night almost felt normal, a night where his grandfather had gone to bed early, and he went out to the patio with his mother and father to watch the sunset. He took his notebook and was able to ask his parents a question he had always wanted to understand the answer to.

But his writing, like his family, is missing something—or better yet, someone—he feels it now, and he knows on the next page it is coming, and like the somber smolder that came over him when he read about the day his girlfriend left, turning the page and starting to read what he wrote twenty days ago makes his insides seize up and ache.

19

The last person to introduce is my sister.

She's somebody who carries with her a heavy, cloud-like sense of emotion. If she's happy and walks into a room, everybody else can feel that happiness, but the same thing can go for sadness and anger. She can freeze a room as much as she can brighten it.

Along with this cloud of emotion, she always wears pear perfume—one of the only traditions we have left from the old country. The recipe for this perfume was written on a folded piece of paper and sewn into the seam of a dress Bubbe wore as she boarded a boat and crossed the sea, not looking back as she left the town in which she was born, to which she would never return, and which would be burned to nothing less than ten years after her departure. Bubbe made the perfume as her mother did and her mother before her, and so on past all memory and record. My mom often says this pear perfume was made by some Tzadik ancestor to remind God of everything beautiful, and to wear this scent was to embody this reminder.

I was never taught the exact recipe, as it's only for the women of the family, but I know the fragrance as well as my own name. I was there the night Bubbe taught my sister to make it, in the same Manhattan apartment where she'd taught my mom so many years earlier. We were on a trip to New York, and on the last night of the trip, while my mom attended some writing event, she left us with Bubbe. I wasn't allowed to learn the recipe but was too young to be left alone, so I stayed close by while Bubbe taught my sister. I remember the smell of pears boiling down on the stove, the sound of Bubbe's accented English slowly describing the steps of distillation while the twinkling light of the whole city shone through the single window of the apartment.

I've looked up to my sister for as long as I've been able to look up to anybody, but we've never been very close. She's almost four years older than me. With this difference in age, we've always lived in slight dissonance: I seem to enter each new stage of life just as she leaves it. When I started middle school, she started high school. When I finally got to high school, she moved to Seattle to go to college and promptly lost touch. Later, we learned that she dropped out through a friend of hers who accidentally told my mom at the supermarket. In the past, when we have tried to connect, we've had a lot of fun, but there haven't been many times like those.

My favorite memories of my sister involve washing dishes after the family dinners my mom used to make on Saturday nights in some sort of conclusion to our peculiar version of Shabbat, which started on Friday night at the nursing home with Zayde. Originally, my sister and I were supposed to alternate washing dishes, but we both hated washing the dishes and constantly fought about whose turn it was. As a result, my parents decided that we would do the dishes together every Saturday night.

It started as something spiteful and tense, each of us hawklike and nitpicking, pointing out specks of food for the other to rewash and mumbling insults under our breath. Pretty quickly, though, in some ways out of necessity, we started having fun, and those minutes in the kitchen together became one of the best parts of each week, at least for me. In the half hour or so when my sister couldn't get in her car or disappear somewhere with her friends, we grew closer than we'd ever been before or have ever been since. It became a time for me to ask questions and maybe get some real insight into what high school held, and maybe the world beyond high school. It became a time for her to tell stories about who she was in love with each week or about her friends and the drama between them.

And in those moments, as the sun set behind us and speckled a brass sheen onto the grey-white tiles of the kitchen and the stainless steel of the sink, in the smell of the lavender soap spread across the room on the steam of the dishwater, laughing together, we felt, if only for a short time, like siblings.

Those minutes in the kitchen, made rusty with the sunset shine, wet-handed and smiling, however, were the exception to our relationship. My sister spent most of her youth out, as my dad often said, "doin' who knows what with who knows who." She was secretive and unpredictable, leaving us guessing as to what she'd do next, like coming home in her junior year of high school with a tattoo of a two-headed snake on her forearm or spending nights away from home without telling our parents where she'd gone, which caused a huge rift between her and my mom.

My mom considers oral processing and deep communication to be an important part of every Jew's life and could never seem to understand my sister's quiet and secrecy. None of us were surprised, but we were nonetheless hurt and upset, when she decided to go to college a couple thousand miles away, rarely reached out in any form, and never once came back for a visit. The whole situation has been a sore spot in the family for years, and even though she and I only text every couple of months, I speak to her more than anybody else in the family. After the Announcement, and before the cell reception went away, we all called her but didn't hear anything back. Even three days after the Announcement, when my dad picked me up, there was still no word from her.

Now, there is a nauseous hush in the air whenever anybody says anything about her. The tears in the fabric of the family she made when she left the way she did have not been repaired over the years, and with the Announcement, what hurt before has been made only worse. Being here, in the house we grew up in, without her, still seeing pictures of the family all together, framed in wood and hung so squarely on the walls, is strange, uncanny even. Without her, the house has felt haunted—not by a presence, but instead by her absence, which makes everything feel crooked and grey.

1

Reading his own description of the feeling of his sister's absence makes the young man shiver as he closes the notebook and walks into the kitchen, where his mom says she was just about to call him to come eat.

For breakfast this morning, as they have had every morning since the young man returned, each family member gets two packets of maple-nut, just-add-water, instant oatmeal. The oatmeal is served in the family's best bowls, which the parents got for their wedding thirty-six years ago. About these bowls, the father decided, "It's the end of the damn world, might as well get a little fancy." One of the defining tastes of this month has been oatmeal. As the father says, "When shit hits the fan, we are gonna have us a hell of a lot of oatmeal, pickles, and cigarettes."

True to his strange taste in stockpiling, for breakfast food the father only bought oatmeal—five palleted and plastic-wrapped bulk cases of maple-nut oatmeal, at that. These boxes are filled with brown paper serving-sized packets, which themselves are filled with dried oats, cane sugar, and crystalized maple flavoring. The nuts in the mix are simply listed as "nuts" on the ingredients section of the package. The family has had a lot of discussions as to what type of nuts these are. At this point, the young man thinks the nuts are almonds because he is pretty sure he saw a whole almond a few days ago, although it may have just been a dried-up cockroach. The mother, too, thinks they are almonds but isn't sure why she thinks so. The father says to ignore the nuts "'cause it's some damn good glop, and it's not like we can look it up online or call the folks who made it to ask," which is something the family has done to settle these petty disputes in the past. The grandfather, when asked what type of nut they were eating, spat bits of oatmeal and grape soda onto the young man's arm while saying, "Atta boy!"

This morning, through the open window in the kitchen, the air outside is already thick and hot, and the sun through the glass is warm like clothes freshly taken out of the dryer. The young man moves a stool into the beam of light so his whole body can soak in this gentle heat, as he is still cold from feeling the absence of his sister, of his girlfriend, and the fast approaching loss of everything else.

The young man's father is making instant coffee with his shirt off. The father always says coffee needs to be "strong enough to float a horseshoe in," and honestly, with the tar-black swill he makes, that might be possible. And thanks to the strength and bite of the father's brew, the air smells like breakfast and the already comfortable light is made even more so. The mother pours packets of oatmeal into a line of fancy bowls on the counter and playfully whips her husband's butt with a dishtowel. The young man does the crossword in one of his mother's old copies of *The New Yorker*, asking her for help with the answers, most of which she knows. The grandfather is sipping grape soda and pacing back and forth between the living room and the dining room, mumbling to himself in Yiddish. The young man used to come over sometimes for breakfast on the weekends, and for a little while this morning, things almost feel like they did back then, even the sound of the dog barking down the street is nearly negligible. The family sits around the kitchen on stools the father made for his wife for Hanukkah last year. The bright day through the windows is made brighter by sunlight reflecting off the kitchen tiles.

The windows in the house are custom made and supposedly can't be shattered by rocks, or even by bullets, according to the father. The house is situated about fifty feet from the street, and there are some large trees and bushes blocking it from sight. Between the house is a reinforced white picket fence. While the street and the city are dangerous these days, and the family constantly hears car alarms, gunshots, yelling, and explosions, they have more or less been unbothered by anybody but themselves and their minds during this time.

And for an hour, things proceed as they usually do, as if nothing is so wrong in the world, as if that world is set to continue indefinitely. The grandfather sips grape soda between bites of oatmeal. The mother reads her favorite book, *The Last of the Just*, writing notes in the margins, which are already filled with notes of different colors from previous readings over the years, as if this book were her own personal Talmud. She chews on the pen cap as she reads and mumbles about the Tzadiks in Yiddish to her father and in English to her son. Meanwhile, the father whistles what sounds like "Jolene" by Dolly Parton, eats his oatmeal straight out of the packet, and mixes some Jack Daniels into his coffee.

1

In the young man's room, the sun enters, gridded through the screen in the window, swirling with dust that shines. The light looks like one of those tchotchkes in small glass bottles sold in long-dead mining towns, full of water and so-called real gold flakes. He sits beside this golden glow alone. And in the loneliness, he is back to thinking of his girlfriend—who seems to still be around him, who sifted his sunlight like the screen does now, like in the Van Zandt song. With her, it was like the soft burn of the stars was pinpointed forward, gathered in her stare and directed toward his chest. And now, when he says her name and hears no reply, when he thinks it or wakes up sweaty after mumbling it in his sleep, he feels like the end can't come soon enough.

She was the light he could see with his eyes closed, the heat beside him, pulsating through the dark. Without her, that brightness and warmth she seemed to hold in her hands, like everything else, is fading. Soon, the raw midday July glare will take over, and the windows will become stinging hot to the touch. It is deep summer now, and he misses her, but winter—could it come again—is when he would miss her the most. Winter was the host of their best slow-motion mornings, staring out over coffee steam at a world of crystaled white. He wishes it was winter, so they could die in the snow, in quiet ice, a muffled numbness waning to nothing. Even fall would be better than summer, for then he could lie on leaves a final time amongst every possible shade of yellow and brown, so close to gold. But none of the young man's wishing matters, as they are in the middle of the hottest summer ever, and the young man's end will be in the heat, in the green and prickly grass of his parents' lawn or on his twin bed with pilling sheets. Tonight, in the middle of the summer, he will die, the husk of something plucked young and set before a great hungry flame.

His headphones are back on now, and Laura Marling's "Night After Night" plays. Eighteen days before, he listened to this very song and wrote about it, what it meant for him, what it reminded him of.

18

My girlfriend played the song I'm listening to right now a long time ago, back when the future held nothing but dreams of our lives together, lives which are now as good as lies.

We were driving through the snow one night a couple of months into our relationship, in what seems like a different world, a different life, a better life. Our relationship felt real in the way something feels real when it isn't new anymore, but is still something you want to keep and hold tight. The snow made everything quiet and a blue sort of bright, even in the darkness. All was cold and still, and we drove slowly on an empty dirt backroad on the outskirts of the city. Like everything outside, we sat in heavy silence. We were having one of our first fights. She put on the song to break this quiet or maybe to change the feeling in the car. Not much time passed before I cried, although I was not quite sure why. My hands quivered, white-knuckled on the steering wheel as Laura Marling sang what I'm hearing now, lyrics that reflect on the passing of time, of watching a lover's body and mind fade away. I think now of all the time she and I won't get to watch each other change, to witness the weight of time shape our bodies, our minds, our everything else.

Marling now sings about sudden shards of light, about fate, about knowing that some end is coming. And maybe now more than ever I understand these lyrics. Maybe she is hoping, as I hope now, that the end will be some gentle and rapid burst of sudden light. Maybe she's saying the real struggle is knowing the end is coming, more than the actual end itself, and sitting in that knowing, trying to make sense of the mess before your waking eyes, trying to live well in the last of the light.

This time of slow rot, the internal grappling with the lack of a tomorrow, is the real torture. It's this knowing that I find awful, and yet somehow a sacred opportunity to get right with something bigger than today, bigger than myself, bigger than the end, something bigger than the knowledge that, even before the Announcement, was always there. That scream of the end of all earthly things. A great light and then the greatest light and then the void. Forever.

As I listen to the song now, I'm brought back to when we were together, long after our first fight, back to when there was so much left of everything, back to when things were better than they had ever been. We used to go on drives at sunset and play this song, remembering how we had made it through together, how we had put so much work and love into our relationship. As the sky was turning colors, after the traffic let up, we took the turns of the dirt road slowly with the windows down. We drove till dark, the song on repeat, watching the gold of the light on each other's faces before the sun sank below sight. Flecks of pollen and clouds of dust stirred by the movement of the car caught the light and turned gold themselves. We drove until we were surrounded by the sepia yellow-white of the plains, the twinkle of house lights and the apartment buildings behind us eating up the black of the night. But in front of us, it was dark enough to see about ten thousand stars, and as we reached the edges of the day, we screamed lyrics into the wind and up toward those pinpricks of white heat so many lifetimes away, suspended as if by magic in the sky.

And as the song crescendos now, my mind turns to a day after my girlfriend left. I was going through the glovebox in my car to find a buck knife I kept in there, just in case. I was standing in the driveway and leaning into the car, my torso stretched across the driver's seat, wind tickling the exposed skin between the folded cuffs of my jeans and my socks.

I glanced up to the windshield on the passenger side and saw faint smudges close to the dashboard. I couldn't tell what they were at first. I leaned forward and looked close and realized these blurs were her footprints, a physical memory of her etched in grease upon the glass. I cried then, like I had the first time I heard the song. That small echo of her set off a sudden burst of cold light in me, like the words of the song, a knowing which broke me open and left me with my legs hanging out of the car into the empty, yellow air.

And these faint traces of her left on my windshield were really the last part of her I ever interacted with. For seventy-two hours after the Announcement—during the day before the night my dad came to take me home—the end of cell service, the internet, and all that came with them was not a question of if, but when. I hoped beyond hope that I would get a call from her before everything was cut off. I hoped that I would have more than her toe prints on my windshield as a last goodbye. I hoped for a call saying everything was okay, that she'd made it home and was with her family and her family's fat cat, who she said was her best friend in the world. A call like so many others I received from her in the last two and a half years, one in which she told me about some trivial thing and how it made her laugh. Hearing that laugh would make everything seem much less heavy.

I sat on the couch, listening to a song about sunlight and daydreams, feeling like both the sun and any dreams were farther away than ever before, waiting for her to sift the air around me, to stir the world back into some sort of normalcy with her laugh. Even if we got cut off mid-conversation and never really got to say a proper goodbye, I didn't want the last interaction I had with her to be watching the bus disappear into that dust-choked sky. My own throat was still choked and aching too. I considered praying, looking up past the ceiling and asking for something, anything, a miracle like that which kept the candles lit so many thousands of years before or parted the sea or left those with blood, like mine, alive. Instead of prayer, I simply waited without speaking, encased in a stale light through the window of the living room in my rental house, my own shadow thin and distant, everything thin and distant.

Then my phone started to vibrate. At first, I thought hope had turned to delusion and made me imagine its movement. Then after the second set of pulses, I figured my unsaid prayer had been answered and I promised to spend the next month believing, even reading the Torah for the first time. I answered, knowing it had to be her reaching out across all those towers and radio waves. I said a shaky "Hello." There was a second of quiet longer than any second before it in the history of time. The air around me burned with a cold, unseen fire.

Then, some robotic voice, glitching and far away, said something like "... sorry to report ... your social security ... immediate attention ... fraud ..." The more the inhuman thing spoke, the less audible the call became. Eventually, the words waned to a high-pitched static. Then, with a faint ringing left in my ears and an empty throbbing left in my gut, cell service went down, followed later that day by the electricity. The darkness in the room made my eyes and temples throb, and I looked up through it to the ceiling, past the ceiling, past that endless, vacant sky, shaking my head.

1

He puts the notebook down, wiping a tear away while trying to find something to distract him from what he has just read and what reading it made him feel. There are many books on the desk where the young man sits after breakfast, taking in the light, recovering from reliving those backroad drives and that day on the couch waiting for a call that never came.

He notices that one of the books on the desk is a copy of *The Old Man and the Sea*, a book he remembers reading when he was a freshman in high school, one of the first books that he really loved, a book which seemed like something more than ink on paper, something that had feeling and movement, something that really had a pulse of its own. He read the whole thing in one day, lying on his parents' couch from waking till dark, so enamored by the images in his head conjured from the letters before his eyes that he forgot to eat. He still remembers the story and how he found in it something stronger than his own hunger. He remembers the scene in the beginning of the book when the old man is getting ready to go out into the dark water, in the same sort of light that always seemed to fill the room when the young man's mother used to tell stories: a soft, butterscotch fog. The young man remembers the end of the story too. The old man prone in his house on the hill, in that same light, after three days at sea, after fighting sharks away from his catch, in the blood and the waves and the deep. The young man remembers the old man on his stiff bed, his hands bloodied, his back and shirt torn open, the boat pulled up onto solid land with the last energy he had left, the townspeople crowded around, holding their hands over gaping mouths, the picked-clean bones of the largest fish anybody has ever seen beside the boat, the sun seeming to split the sky open with its fire, shining over this great victory. The young man remembers how despite all the battles and small losses in this book, the old man, a

Tzadik, a holy fool, remains glorious even in defeat. A certain passage comes to the young man's mind, something he still holds on to: *It is easy when you are beaten, he thought. I never knew how easy it was. And what beat you? he thought, "Nothing," he said aloud.*

And the young man feels that he, too, has been beaten, torn apart by the Announcement and its aftermath, and he hopes that there will be some ease in his defeat. He hopes he can find the ease that the old man did, even after losing everything he worked so hard to hold in his hands.

He has always wanted to be part of a larger story like this, to live like a character in a book where something spectacular happens. Instead, for most of his life, he awakened to a cool morning, followed by work or study or errands and a night spent readying himself for another day of the same. He thought with everything that has happened, all the loss and aimless hours, that he would have let go of his wish to face a great challenge and overcome it, but this desire to live a life worthy of stories has not gone away—if anything, he feels it more now. He wishes to have in his life, like there is in all his favorite stories, conflict, climax, resolution, twists and turns and wacky hijinks along the way. But somewhere in him, he knows that his is simply the story of a family waiting for the end, simply trying to make it through another day until there are no days left.

Still, the young man can't help but wish there were some great and evil thing, red-eyed and lurking, something to fight, something to challenge for the fate of the world. In every story that has drawn him into its folds, there has been some triumph against clear evil, some salvation, some sense of hope and survival, at least. Despite torture at the hands of the Nazis and their many predecessors, in the end and in birthing brightness, the just ones, the Tzadiks, made it through. And the young man wants this for himself, and his family too, but he knows in the deep of his belly that they cannot fight this coming night and the nothing that will follow.

He tries to remember the words of that passage, the ease of being beaten, the letting go of trying to win, the surrendering to the flood of flames, the breathing of deep breaths before there will no longer be any breathing at all.

And readying himself toward the end, he opens the notebook again and reads the next page, facing his past, so he can face the splinter which remains of the future.

15

After high school, I didn't want to commit myself to years of study and debt, so while I waited to see what I was going to do with the rest of my life, a bunch of years passed, and in that time I worked at a farm. I'd never worked at a farm before, nor would I have guessed that a farm is where I would end up, but that is how it went, and I guess how it often goes. You arrive somewhere you never would've imagined yourself, and you try to make the best of it. Before working there, I had no idea how to coax stem and blossom from the dirt, how or when to plant, how to weed or prune or harvest, but I'd worked construction with my dad since I was old enough to lift a barrow of dirt and move it across a jobsite, so I was strong and able and knew the value and feeling of working with my hands.

I became interested in working at a farm after going to a lecture my mom gave about the history of Jews and land, the history of a deep connection that had been stolen through war and genocide and exile. She described how some young Jews were returning to the land, learning how to farm, to be with the earth in a way that our forefathers had been robbed of by so many thousands of years of displacement.

I was fascinated by a story my mom told during her lecture about a rabbi from nearly four hundred years ago, a man credited with the founding of Hasidism and who came from the same Ashkenazi blood that runs through my own veins, a man called the Baal Shem Tov. This man, along with so many other things, wanted Jews to move out from the dusty synagogues, to get their noses out of books, to get their hands in the ground, to grow a world of their own under a golden sun. But during this rabbi's time, and for so long before and after, Jews were not allowed to own much—or any—land. My mom mulled over the fact that while the rituals and rites of Judaism and much of our religious law is connected to the seasons, diaspora Jews were nevertheless unable to connect to or make a home upon the ground beneath their feet for so long. I found it hard to follow all the history, to be honest, but one thing I was clear on was that I needed to get my hands in the dirt. My mom concluded her lecture by describing this new generation of Jews, allowed to stand on the ground and not be moved, to be somewhere on their own terms for once and to make that place bloom. The day after the lecture, after telling my girlfriend about the spark that had been lit in my heart hearing about Jews and our relationship to the earth, she told me she had a friend who worked at a farm and that this friend had recently mentioned they were hiring. I phoned the farm that evening, and in three days I was on my knees in a row of white flowers, pulling up strangleweed with my bare hands and feeling closer to a home, to a purpose, than I ever had.

I worked away the summers at the farm, sweating, pulling weeds, sweating even more, sorting and washing and bagging produce, and hauling compost. Those of the workers who could tan got many shades darker, some of us getting such bad t-shirt tans it looked like we were wearing white tees when we had our shirts off. Twice a week, we drove about an hour to a farmer's market to sell what we had grown and trade for what we hadn't with booths representing other farms. We saved money during the summer, and when winter came we lived off what we had saved, resting our aching legs and backs, our sunburned necks, our hands as hard as the rocks we pulled from the veggie beds.

At the farm we had a tradition of growing our hair out for the entirety of the summer, and those of us who could grow beards grew them out as well. We started the season in April with a ceremonial night before the first sowing. In the barn, we took turns shaving each other's heads and necks and faces with an electric razor. The collective hair swirled and piled up, straight and curly and brown and black and blonde and red and grey on the dirt at our feet. The next day, we placed the first sprouts in the still-cold ground, wearing hats and hoods and scarves around our freshly hairless heads. During this time, we wondered aloud why tradition involved us having no hair in the coldest parts of the year and a lot of hair in the heat, but still, we repeated this tradition each spring. We let our hair grow as the plants grew; what came from our heads and faces was as long as the sprouts of cabbage and chard and lettuce and beets when they finally poked out of the ground.

And as in the past, this April before the first sowing, I shaved my face and head along with everybody else, and even though the farm closed after the Announcement, my hair has been growing since. It now covers my whole forehead and hangs at the top edges of my vision. There are little golden ringlets, which spindle themselves at the borders of my face and neck. I have a beard, which is at least three fingers long and much darker than the hair on my head. I think often of all these people with whom I spent summers sweating in the sun. I think of the dry dirt we helped heal back into healthy soil, the sprouts we eased into blossom and fruit, how all of that now is just waste and weeds again, as if we'd never spent so many months on our hands and knees working as if in prayer. I don't know where the people I worked with and for are. I hope they're safe somewhere with people they love. What I do know is that today I still carry the remnants of a tradition, the beginnings of a community that felt like something from a time long before this. Within me, in the calluses on my hands and the almost permanent dirt under my nails, I carry pieces of that place now vacant and overgrown.

1

As he flips to the next page, the young man unconsciously runs his hands through his hair, twists his fingers in his unkempt beard, and sighs with the weight of yet another lost thing. This notebook seems to be little more than a catalog of loss. But in that loss, he feels a warmth too, a knowledge that despite the stunted timeline of his life, he has felt much love and has had things to lose, and in some ways, the writing and the reading of this notebook has helped him to understand that, to justify his life to himself. Feeling this match tip of warmth and light against the darkness of all that has happened and is to come, he continues to read and feels the beginnings of something like peace.

14

For so long I've wanted a place to make my own, not just for myself, but in which I can create a container of safety and community for those I love, my own soil, something to put my hands into, siding to paint whatever color I want and replace when it's old—a kitchen where I'm the only one leaving dirty dishes in the sink, a bathtub stained with only my grime. But the likelihood of being able to afford a house was slim on account of the low pay at the farm and the rising cost of living everywhere. Now, after the Announcement, I know I'll never have the place I imagined for as long as I've been able to imagine anything. However, in my garden, for maybe the first time in my life, I have the beginning of a place where I can create the world I want for myself and those I love, some earth to till and sow. And in that, there's something sacred, my own translation of the Baal Shem Tov's ideas into seed and soil, my own turn in history, my own return to the land.

Two years ago, I built my garden in my parents' back yard because there was no yard in the house I used to rent. I knew my parents had wanted a garden for a long while but never had time to build one. I figured everyone could get something they wanted in one afternoon of my sweat. I built the garden with old boards I was allowed to take from a construction site I helped my dad work on. The boards were painted a light blue and had small holes and tool marks on them from when they were part of a house with a faulty foundation. The boards were sturdy and weatherworn, and most importantly, they were free. I cut these two-by-twelve lengths of heavy, salvaged wood into two lengths of five feet and two lengths of ten feet. Then I screwed the lengths into four four-by-four posts and set them at the corners. I filled the frame of the box with a few truckloads of dirt I took from another one of my dad's jobsites and topped it with some compost and mulch I was able to take from the giant piles we had at the farm.

I dug each inch-deep hole for the seeds in rows with my bare fingers. The soil was soft and healthy and cool and smelled like earth and moss and, as I planted the first seeds, I understood the medicine of the soil, of place, of home. There, in that frame of dirt and old wood and soon to be sprouting seed, everything was suddenly okay. Even though I spent my workdays weeding and planting and working in the dirt, I still made time to come to my parents' house to manage the garden. Something felt different about having my own space, my own land to tend, even if it was just fifty square feet in my parents' back yard. There, I could disappear. I understood what the Baal Shem Tov spoke of, what my mom discussed in her lecture: the true happy place is the holy place, the feeling of God outside of the stuffy synagogue or the office or the university library, the feeling of God with the sun on my neck and my hands in the dirt, the feeling of God in the garden and how that is the truest of homes.

Today, this rectangle of earth is so different than it once was. I've already had two harvests from my garden this year, one of radishes, lettuce, and cabbage, another of peas, and I'm currently growing my third. There are six tall cherry tomato plants bent with fruit, some of which will never ripen. Cucumbers consume the back left corner and are starting to climb up the fence. Carrots and beets of various sizes and shapes and colors poke deep into the ground and sprout purple and green sprays of leaves into the air. There are now the beginnings of a pumpkin and three shiny Japanese eggplants ready for picking. There are white butterflies and fat, fuzzy bumblebees, moving in ways that seem impossible according to the laws of physics. In the back right corner of the garden, my girlfriend planted tobacco jasmine, which blooms at night, marigolds, which help keep pests away from the tomato plants, and an assortment of other types of stems and petals, which span the spectrum of color and scent. Her favorite flowers were sunflowers, and she planted as many seeds as she could, but somehow not a single bud has yet come up.

And today, needing a break from the indoors, I spent many happy hours in my garden, this fifty-square-foot expanse of life, of which I'm the steward and which stewards me as much I do it, in which I feel closer and more connected to the sacred. With my hands in the dirt and the sun warming the back of my neck, I fell into a familiar trance. The barks of the dog down the street became barely audible as I focused on the feelings of the soil and the sunlight on my skin and the smell of the flowers in the hot, lazy wind.

1

The mother made a strict schedule for these last four weeks. She says the schedule was there to provide something to look forward to, to hold onto through the day, so they don't get bogged down with whatever heaviness comes from what she will only refer to as "our situation." Breakfast at eight thirty, lunch at twelve thirty, dinner at seven, and there are pickles pretty much everywhere if they need any snacks. The young man has done his best to adhere to these mealtimes, but sometimes he forgets where he is supposed to be, lost in sorrow or soil or something else. Maybe he seeks distraction, tries to forget the time—how little of it he has left. He is often late to the table.

When the children were growing up, the only time they ate together was on Saturday night, after which the two siblings washed the dishes together. Now, the family eats together more than ever before, and according to a stricter routine, for several reasons: It is a way to break up the day and a way to spend time with one another. It is also a way to forget about what is coming. Eating is something they do together, something to pull them out of their rooms or their heads, where they often retreat when they are not compelled to their places at the table. Now, after reading about his garden, his humble source of food and home, the young man is inspired to go spend some time there before lunch, in this place where he forgets about nearly everything, including the schedule and even, for brief moments, the end of the world.

The return to the work in the earth makes him melt away momentarily, but taken from this bliss by a particularly loud bark from down the street, he comes to, realizing he is probably late for lunch. He jogs barefoot over the scratchy grass, through the beating-down sun, and goes inside.

1

Most years, his father "gets himself an elk," resulting in another nearly hundred pounds of meat in the freezer. Presently, there are about two hundred pounds of elk meat stockpiled in two chest freezers in the garage. The young man doesn't love the gamey taste of elk, but he is grateful they have so much of it, as it has kept the family going more than once. There have been times in the winter, when the farm was closed and his nest egg was running low, that he survived off of his father's elk meat. Also, when the children were younger and their mother was an assistant professor and their father did not yet own his own company, the young man can remember eating a diet of mostly elk and boxed mac and cheese. Eventually, his parents started to make more money, but nonetheless, one of the staples of the family diet has always been a seemingly endless supply of elk jerky, elk steaks, elk burgers, elk sausages, and any other elk meat byproduct the father can make in the garage. So, as they have had every other day for lunch, today they are having elk burgers.

Each member of the family has contrived unique ways of making the elk burgers edible. The grandfather happily chomps between sips of grape soda, mumbling things like "Atta boy" and phrases in Yiddish, which make the mother crack up but which she rarely decides to translate. The mother eats her burger without a bun, cut up into bite-sized pieces, which she usually dips in mustard of some sort. The father will do what he calls a double stack, layering two patties on top of each other with a layer of cheese and ketchup and so on between the patties, as well as between the buns. Each day, the father makes the same joke about how he might bust his jaw trying to take his first bite, but somehow, he doesn't. The young man's favorite thing to do is put french fries, if they have any, in the stack of meat and veggies between the buns. Since the family only had enough bags of frozen french fries to have them once per week, in honor of some sort of Shabbat they decided to only eat fries on Fridays, a day which the father named "French Fry-days." And although today is not Friday, they saved the only bag of tater tots they had in the freezer for lunch today, because there will be no tomorrow and it has given them something to look forward to. The young man comes inside and washes his hands with the lavender dish soap by the sink. He walks toward the table where everybody is eating. On the table is a salad made from veggies he grew in his garden, two jars of pickles, one of which is almost finished, a bowl of tater tots, a plate of buns, and a plate of elk burgers. After the first jar of pickles is finished, as has happened almost every day, the grandfather drinks the remainder of the juice while the family all looks the other way. The young man now takes the last burger from the serving plate. He layers tots on top of his burger, as well as a bit of the salad and some ketchup. He squishes it down into a bite-able mass and takes a massive first bite.

He nearly spits it out. The patty is extremely charred, as if it had been set on fire and left to burn for at least a minute before being put out. He is not very picky, but if he is picky about one thing, it is charred food. He didn't always hate charred food, but he started to after he helped his father do some demolition at a house that had burned down. He spent two weeks during a high school summer hauling charred dirt and broiled-looking boards to a dumpster for eight hours a day. The whole time he worked, all he could smell or taste was ash. His hands were stained black for weeks and his hair changed colors for a while thanks to the dark and clinging dust. Since that summer, he hasn't been able to stomach the least bit of charcoal on food. The first bite of burnt burger takes him momentarily back to when the tips of his fingernails were pitch black and there was a tasteless grey in every pore.

The young man asks his mother if she wants to switch burgers with him, but she has already cut hers into pieces and eaten about half. So has everybody else. The young man deconstructs the layers of meat, bread, tots, sauce, and vegetables onto his plate. Then, he takes the patty in his hand and walks to the sink. As he is going to the kitchen to deal with the burger, there is a ringing frustration in his ears, and his hands are shaking.

Trying to focus on making things better instead of on what is to come and the rushing feeling of how soon midnight will arrive, the young man tries to scrape the black and flaky char from the patty with a butter knife. While standing at the sink, he can hear muffled giggles from his mother, amused by some story his father is telling and the sound of his grandfather's noshing.

As fast as everything changed from normal to ruined with the bite of the charred burger, the full weight of the end of the world comes down on him in a split second. This weight comes in waves. Sometimes he is fine, and then overwhelming hopelessness and defeat rolls in. There at the sink he experiences the deepest hopelessness he has felt since the few minutes after the bus carrying his girlfriend disappeared into the dusk. As he tries to scrape the burger down to something edible and not gag at the smell of the burn swirling in the air, his knees grow weak and his head starts to spin. His mouth is sticky and dry. His hands lose their grip, and he drops both the burger and the butter knife into the sink. For a few moments, he is elsewhere, gone from his skin, swimming in despair.

The burger makes a soft clunk as it comes into contact with the stainless steel, and the knife makes a metallic bang, which brings the young man back into his body. He takes stock of the present in an attempt to calm himself. He is standing in the kitchen, his parents' kitchen. The dog down the street is barking, as it has been for so long. He tries to let the sound ground him. He exhales and inhales. He holds the edge of the sink with both hands, like it is the only thing stopping him from a great fall.

From the other room, the mother asks if everything is alright. He says he is fine as he takes the burger from the wet steel and walks out the backdoor. He strides across the coarse grass, squinting in the summer sun and tosses the burger as hard as he can over the fence toward the sound of the barking. There is no break in the sound.

The young man tells himself that he needs to keep it together for the sake of his family. When he gets back to the screen door, he can see his mother standing in the kitchen, looking out into the day. Raising her eyebrows, she asks what's going on. He opens the door and walks past her, saying he has decided to have ice cream for lunch. "Don't," she says. He responds, "Why not? We're dying today. It's not like it matters if I don't have a solid lunch or if my stomach hurts from the dairy." She raises her eyebrows even higher and tells him, "Well, for one, you get cranky when you don't have a solid meal, and for two, I don't want you to spend the rest of the day upset, and for three, I thought we agreed not to give up on trying to be positive and act as normal as we can, and for four… Well, I guess I only have three points." The young man reminds himself that despite the world ending tonight, he needs to try to make things okay, that maybe just being okay for now is the most righteous thing he can do. He says, "You're right. I'm sorry. Sometimes I just can't act normal." The mother and son stand there without saying anything for a second, and then the young man continues, "But I'm still going to eat ice cream."

He takes a spoon from the drawer to the left of the sink, turns, and opens the freezer. He pulls out a pint of pralines and cream. He sinks his spoon in, brings it to his lips and then into his mouth, and closes his eyes. He feels the melting of the ice cream on his tongue, the sugar going straight to his head. His bliss is interrupted by his mother saying, "Fuck it," which is a rare utterance from her. She grabs a spoon and takes a pint of mango sorbet from the freezer. The father comes into the kitchen saying, "What in tarnation is goin' on here?" And when he sees what they are doing, he grabs himself a spoon and a pint of rocky road, saying he has to have a flavor that matches the type of street he grew up on. The mother calls to her father in Yiddish, presumably asking if he wants any ice cream. He responds with a slurping, which could have come from either a soda can or a pickle jar.

Barefoot on the tile, the mother, the father, and the son take big bites of ice cream straight from their individual pints. The young man feels like he has inadvertently brought some joy to this last lunch, and in that he feels as though he has done something at least slightly righteous. The hands of the family are wet from the melting frost on the ice cream cartons. The condensation drips down and puddles on the floor, but nobody notices the mess. They smile at one another. The sky outside is blue and cloudless and looks painted onto the very edge of the world.

1

With the dog down the street constantly barking and waking him earlier than he wants to wake up, the young man has started taking naps in the afternoon. When he is sleeping, he does not think about the end of the world. He loves the feeling of coming to, and for a moment lying still in the bliss of not knowing what has happened or what will happen, before it comes crushingly back. As he too quickly remembers the situation, he feels like his family and the whole world has died before dying, that what happened to start out this month has been more of an end than what will come tonight.

When he sleeps now, he does not dream, and he thinks that the end and all the loss it has created has dulled his subconscious.

Besides his dreams, one of the things the young man misses from his old life is the sticky notes that his girlfriend would leave for him to find. They had quotations on them meant to inspire him throughout his day. She kept a stack of yellow sticky notes and a purple ballpoint pen in her bag or purse or pocket in case somebody in her life needed handwritten motivation—as the young man often did. He kept the notes she left him throughout the years, the I's dotted with hearts and the L's and Y's and J's and G's looped. He keeps these notes in a wooden box his father made for him when he was younger to hold pens and pencils. This box is one of the few things he took from his rented house when he returned home.

Sitting in his room after his post-lunch nap, after having awakened to the sound of the dog once again barking, the young man crawls across the bed, sits at the desk, opens the box of notes, and picks one at random, hoping that whatever comes out can serve as a message from her and guide the rest of his day:

> "Write it on your heart that every day is the best day in the year. He is rich who owns the day, and no one owns the day who allows it to be invaded with fret and anxiety. Finish every day and be done with it. You have done what you could. Some blunders and absurdities, no doubt crept in. Forget them as soon as you can, tomorrow is a new day; begin it well and serenely, with too high a spirit to be cumbered with your old nonsense. This new day is too dear, with its hopes and invitations, to waste a moment on the yesterdays."
>
> –Ralph Waldo Emerson

The quotation is so long it takes up both sides of the sticky note. The last line is squished in tiny, illegible writing at the bottom of the back side. He has to ask his mother if she knows the rest of it. Of course, his mother recites the missing piece from memory for the young man to digest.

Now he is back at the desk, looking at the note written in a hand he wishes were here to hold his own. He can't remember when she gave him this sticky note, but for the last twenty minutes or so, he has tried to take the words to heart.

These words have such a different meaning than they must have before, but really, it is the woman behind the words that he thinks of while he reads, trying to ignore the fact that there will be no new day to hold dear. All he has are the yesterdays with her and these notes in a pine box in his old room at the end of his young life. Beside the boxful of her handwritten words is an empty pack of the same sticky notes she used. He misses the way she could make so much out of a yellow square, using only the magic of her fingers and a pen. Without her, the places she would have filled and made better are left empty, like so much has been left empty in the last thirty days. But then he thinks that she has surely filled other places, far away, and in doing so, brought joy to others. After reading the note, he opens his notebook, determined to get through all he has written before the evening, before what will come at the end of the day.

12

I miss the days when I used to wake up late, stumble into the living room rubbing my eyes, and spread out on the couch. I miss days when there was nothing to do and no guilt around not doing anything. Recently, I haven't been able to relax and have felt the need to make use of every moment, to make everything I do have a clear sense of purpose.

But this has been the least productive month of my life, and the sort of nothing I've been doing has been the worst sort. Every footfall or breath exhaled in a sigh has been tainted by the knowledge that everything is that much nearer to the last. The pressure to make use of the time has made me feel less motivated to do anything, and I simultaneously get mad at myself for not being motivated then feel less motivated by having to deal with the added pressure of feeling mad about not doing anything. This goes on and on, and it will until the end, I suppose, this cycle of doing nothing in an attempt to do it all. I miss feeling like there were endless days—but of course no one really has that. Every person's days are numbered, but somehow before all this it felt possible that things could go on forever. I realize now that there never were endless days; there never were infinite chances to wake up and watch the world polish the ceiling in yellow window shapes. So I guess what I miss isn't the endlessness, but the illusion of it. I've spent a lot of time in the past month watching movies, which makes me feel like I should be doing something different—more productive or better—but I remain in front of the TV all the same. It isn't safe to leave the confines of the house or the back yard, and there are only so many things to do or say in either of those places.

And when I say that I've watched a lot of movies, what I really mean is that I've watched the same two movies many times. When I was growing up, we had a DVD player and a huge collection of movies, however, due to the advent of streaming and to us children moving out and Mom trying to get rid of things, my parents donated the DVD player and the collection of DVDs a few years back. But in this disconnected month back in the house together, we suddenly faced the void of the entertainment which used to fill the shelves in the living room. After a frantic search for something to watch other than the emergency signal broadcasting on all 8,000 channels, reminding the world of the Announcement, I was able to find four movies on VHS.

In the closet of the bedroom that used to be mine, then wasn't, and now is again, I found *Shrek* and *An American Tale*. I got *Shrek* for Hanukkah whenever it came out. My grandparents, via my mom, gave me and my sister *An American Tale* when we were very young as a way for us to understand our Grandparents' stories as Ashkenazi immigrants. Sadly, *An American Tale* has a couple of big skips in it that have made it unwatchable. In my sister's room, I found *Wayne's World* and *Schindler's List*. I hated going into my sister's room and felt the scream of the silence in there, but I braved it on the chance there was something else to watch. I found a VCR in the garage, tucked behind a stack of toilet paper and jars of pickles. Miraculously, I also found the precise combination of cables I needed to rig it to the TV in the living room.

Wayne's World was not as funny as I remembered, but I've watched it over ten times, so much so that my mom put a moratorium on quoting it. *Shrek* was great—bad yet good, that sort of great. I'm also not allowed to quote *Shrek* since my dad came out into the garden when I was doing some weeding and I told him to "Get out of my swamp!" which my dad found funny but which my mom has grown tired of hearing. I've now seen *Shrek* and *Wayne's World* so many times that I play a game with myself when I watch them in which I try to say as many consecutive lines as I can without messing up or forgetting. The record for *Shrek* is thirty-six minutes of nonstop quoting, and the record for *Wayne's World* is twenty-three minutes.

If I had more time, I think I would write a personality quiz book based on the *Shrek* soundtrack with a hypothesis that whichever song you liked as a child defined your life. I remember that my sister's favorite song detailed how the singer didn't care about the bad reputation she had, which I feel like set my sister up for a life of rebellion and wild haircuts and being gone.

My favorite song from the soundtrack is the cover of Leonard Cohen's "Hallelujah." When I was given *Shrek*, I was also given the CD and used to read the lyrics and listen to that song on repeat. The lyrics were the first to move me and make me realize that songs could be stories and that these stories could guide my life, and they inspired me to look deeper into Cohen's work. It was also meaningful to me that Cohen was a Jew. I liked that he was a Jew because, at the time, I was the only Jew in my class at school, and I was under the impression, based on what my classmates said, that Jews were all weak and dorky and lame. But when I found that song and did some research on Cohen and saw how cool and creative and beloved he was, I felt like I too could maybe be okay even though I was Jewish. In my research, I found "The Partisan," a song about Jews who took to the woods and fought against the Nazis, fought back against annihilation, and through Cohen I learned of the strength of the tribe we belong to, of an enduring flame, of something that burned in him and still burns in me.

I mostly watch movies at night, alone and a little drunk, after everyone else has gone to bed, but one early afternoon about a week ago, we all decided to watch *Schindler's List*. We had it on for less than ten minutes before we turned it off and swore not to watch it again. It just felt too real—the bleakness, the empty faces, the empty sky, the end of so many. There seemed no use in seeing another awful thing. Despite the agreement to not watch it anymore, my mom has watched it a few more times since. She's cried on and off throughout the film while I sulked around the house, watching snippets in passing.

And maybe it's a cliché for a bunch of Jews to be crying and watching *Schindler's List* at the end of the world, but it's one of the four movies we had, and also it's a story that holds true in ways that I never expected. What I think made me uncomfortable and made my mom break down was that, back then, there were people that could help, there were little blips of color in the darkness, there was a chance, albeit small, for a way out. Now, there seems to be no color left, and the hours wane to ash.

The only other videos that we have here are some home videos my mom found in her closet: a video of my parents' wedding and others of me and my sister when we were younger, jumping on my parents' bed, building snowmen and riding on a bright red sled that looks neon in the snow, and other classic childhood scenes. While remembering those days as a group and hearing my dad make jokes over his own wedding tape and tell wild stories about the people who were there may sound fun at the same time, the idea of watching those videos makes us all feel a little sick. Seeing everybody, including my sister, so wide-eyed and together and simple and smiling and full of hope, with lives and worlds ahead of us, is too much to bear, so we haven't watched the home movies. Yet they sit below the TV and catch my eye every time I walk by, calling out to be seen.

Other than movies to help pass these long and sacred empty days, we have a deck of cards, but none of us can remember any games other than Go Fish and Solitaire, both of which got old pretty fast. My mom has Scrabble, but she knows so many more words than everybody else that it isn't really fun to play with her. So in these, the last weeks of living—which we want so desperately to move quickly but also wish would never end—we've mostly just had each other to pass the time with.

1

The young man flips to the next page in the notebook and realizes that he accidently left two pages blank before the next entry. He decides to fill that gap in his chronicle now.

The end and its wide wave of fire are coming, but the family is too afraid to discuss it openly. The young man fears that bringing up the specifics of the promised end could wreck what little peace and composure they have left, so instead he daydreams, working through the end on his own. In the musty quiet of his bedroom, in the early afternoon as his mother reads, his grandfather naps, and his father gets ready to take a bath, the young man writes about how the world *might* end, what he'd like to happen if he could choose right now:

> I take off running in bare feet. The grass splays beneath my sprint and is cold on my skin, frigid in the way grass gets during the summer at night. I clear the fence between my parents' back yard and then the fence beyond the neighbor's house and the house beyond that, hopping fences until I reach the yard where the barking dog lives. I land hard on white dirt, kicking up dust like chalk, scraping a hole through my blue jeans and the skin of my knee. I stand, my knee clotted with a grey sludge of blood and pale dirt. Dark drips of blood move down the inside of my pants, cooling around the elastic of my sock, soaking the white cotton to the point that, with each step I take, there is a wet sound. I don't worry about the stain or the damage done. There is no use in that now.
>
> The yard is sparse, mainly white dirt, dog shit, and a few clumps of grass so white and dry they look like they are made of plaster. The fence is chain-link, and the metal diamonds are coiled with the same strangleweed that I pull out in handfuls from the farm where I worked—and

> from my garden as well. This invasive green is the only color in the yard, everything else is parched white. I look around after standing, trying to breathe through the throbbing, stinging pulse in my knee. Pawsteps then, light on the soft dirt but not small. The light of the margarine moon right before midnight is shadowed and fractured by tree leaves and telephone wire. The animal approaches through the black-and-white night. I first recognize the dog by its tail, by the way it bends off to the side where it was broken: the origin of *tragicute*. I'm tackled then, but not in attack. Tongue kisses wet my face. I pet her head as we wait together for the break in the black and then the nothing that will follow the light.

And as the young man sets down his pen, he supposes this would be a half decent end. A full circle. A storybook ending in which a miracle occurs and the dog he and his girlfriend wanted is miraculously present, near to his home.

But when he thinks further, he sees that it is her he wants, the one who revealed to him all the tragicuteness of the world. Not an emblem or symbol of her in the form of the dog, but the woman herself, the one he calls to mind with every *she* and *you* and *love* in the songs he knows best. So he turns to the second blank page and starts to write again, a vision of an end he would be happy to face, which he knows will not come, but which, in the minutes he is writing it, are made real:

> I'm in my car with my girlfriend, tightly holding hands, the spaces between my fingers filled with hers. The sunset is ongoing, looking like the whole sky is on soft fire. The broken sunroof of my silver car is somehow working and open and letting in fast, sweet-smelling air as we drive. The air is pink and white and gold. The clouds are thin and warm. My foot is pressed hard on the gas. The music is turned all the way up. A song ripples through the speakers, something with acoustic guitar

> and sad lyrics, yet somehow hopeful and endless. I've always thought "Fast Car" by Tracy Chapman would be a good song to listen to while driving into the sunset. So, yes, that song is playing, and I put my arm around her shoulder, and the city lights are behind us, and the whole glow of the rest of the world and the sinking sun spread like a color palette in front of the car, and in that very moment we go, and we are free of hurt, full of each other and the floral air soaring through the windows.
>
> The last thing we see is a wave of holy splendor that sweeps so gently and quickly and soundlessly across the plains. A landscape lit by the likes of twenty thousand suns, which fade to perfect white, then away.

As he finishes writing, he feels that the fire he was writing about is burning within him. He sits in that glow and the warmth of that fire, hoping that wherever she is, she is somehow feeling it too.

1

There are so many things the young man could have done this month. He could have read every book he has ever been recommended. He could have painted, or he could have danced and sung or walked downtown to the local art museum and stolen any painting he wanted. Instead, he wrote, worked in his garden, spent time with his family, and listened to all his favorite songs. After the initial shock of the Announcement, there was not much to do other than be around the people he loved. Nothing else seemed to matter, and it is in this mode of being, this communal feeling, that he has decided he wants to die: he wants to be together for as much of the rest of the day as he can. After detailing the dramatic scene of riding off into the sunset to die, he feels guilty for not spending the whole day with his family. But the pull of the writing is real. He struggles against it, and at last he is able to quell the urge to read more of what he has written, instead going out to the patio where his grandfather is sitting.

After the sun is hidden by the roof of the house, it is somewhat breathable in the shade. The young man has taken to testing how many times he can walk around the wooden four-by-fours framing the flagstone of the patio without falling off. They are skinny enough, and he is distracted easily enough, that he has been unable to go the full way around without falling. While he tries to balance, he will talk with whoever is on the patio. If his grandfather is out there, even though he probably doesn't understand, the young man usually tells him a story from his life, about the place he used to go dancing with his girlfriend or the farm where he used to work. It feels nice to tell his grandfather about his life, and he thinks his grandfather likes it too, because he nods along and smiles a yellow-toothed grin. As the young man speaks, sometimes he will gesture to his grandfather to toss him a pickle, and sometimes his grandfather will understand. A couple days ago, the young man tried to get his grandfather to open the jar and throw him one, but he simply tossed the entire jar at the young man and it shattered on the ground. The stain of the brine is still visible on the flagstone, and a dried-up pickle is nudged against the beams, another casualty of mistranslation.

Today, his grandfather sucks at a cigarette and a can of grape soda, wearing a cardigan despite the day being throat-cloggingly dry and bright. The mother comes out and sits beside her father on one of the weather-whitened chairs next to the glass table in the center of the flagstone. The grandfather says something to his daughter in Yiddish, and they both laugh. She takes a cigarette from the turquoise pack on the table.

The young man's mother loves to discuss writing and philosophy and Jewish history, and the young man wishes he had spent more of his life educating himself to be like her. It is wonderful to pick her brain in a casual manner about topics of little urgency, but every once in a while she wants to talk about something pressing. The young man can tell when his mother has something serious to say by the way she looks when she walks into a room. It is something about the way she puts up her hair and the way her eyes get small and turn from light blue to darker blue like the twilit sky. She had her hair up in this way and her eyes tight and azure when she came outside just now, and the young man can tell they are about to get into one of those conversations. But as usual, the mother takes her time when she wants to bring something up, so she comes out like nothing is on her mind and starts smoking. This, in itself, is revealing because she only smokes when she is anxious. But she smokes her cigarette as if everything in the whole wide world is perfect and smiles at both her father and her son.

The young man and his mother and grandfather talk about the weather and other trivial things with her translating between large puffs of smoke. When she finishes her first cigarette, she puts it out straight onto the glass of the table and motions for her father to give her another, to which he says, "Nope," but obliges. She lights her second cigarette and leans back in her chair, trying to act like everything is okay. The young man, still balancing on the beams that frame the patio, politely asks his mother to spit out whatever she needs to say, explaining it kills him to have to wait for her to talk. The mother looks up at her son as her father sips his grape soda loudly, and from beyond the fence surrounding the back yard the dog barks every few seconds, the howls turning to whines at the end of each breath. The parts of the lawn that are still in direct sun look shriveled and mean.

The mother sighs, and smoke flows out of her mouth. From the beam where he is balanced, the young man watches the smoke rise toward the sky and meet with harsh light. When his eyes meet the sky, he sees there are no contrails from airplanes crisscrossing the blue. This might be the most obvious visible change since the Announcement: the clarity of the sky. It's not the first time he has noticed this. In fact, he notices it most days—the sky, so empty and bright—but despite the fact that it is not the first time he has noticed it, this new emptiness of the sky still gives him chills and reminds of the end soon to come. As he thinks about airplanes and how he won't see one or its stream of cloud ever again, he slips off the beam and walks back to the start to begin a new attempt at going all the way around.

His mother draws deeply on her cigarette and finally speaks up, She continues, "I want to talk now about the end of the world, but not only the one we are facing tonight." The young man says "go ahead" as he starts to walk around the beams again. His mother says, "after I am done I want to hear what you are feeling, the scene at lunch worried me." The young man agrees but in his head wonders what the point of saying how he feels would be when there are only eight hours left of life.

His mother begins "There is this thing called historical trauma, in which bad things that have happened to our ancestors are passed down through DNA. These things show up from one generation to another, remnants of slavery or genocide, proof of how even from birth—if not before—everyone is made of history.""But," his mother goes on, "one definition of a trauma is simply being overwhelmed. This got me thinking that while one can be overwhelmed by sadness and pain, one can also be overwhelmed by happiness and good feelings. Maybe there is some such thing as generational knowing or generational joy. Maybe, somewhere deep inside our bones, beyond our bones even, beyond our blood, people hold everything done and felt by the people who made us: all our great loves and sacred triumphs. Within us, each person holds the glory of everybody they come from. Inside of us, each person carries all people who have come before. I realized that my writing is not only my own, it is also the product of so many generations of rabbis and thinkers, including those who never had the opportunity to write or those whose writing and words have been lost." Looking at the young man directly, she says, "Your farm work is, likewise, the product of accumulated wisdom: so many people in the past working in the ground under the sun on kibbutzim and on what little land Jews were allowed to cultivate. Everything everybody is, is so much more than just a moment in time or a single person, everybody is a mix of everybody who made them and all that they carried and held dear."

As she speaks and smokes, the grandfather lights cigarettes for himself and the dog barks lazily at the empty sky. The father fiddles with his HAM radio in the garage, and on the patio they can hear occasional static. They sit in a square of warm shadow cast by the house, and outside the shadow the light is white and scorching.

The mother exhales a plume of white-grey smoke and says she "Jews have lived through so many ends before, and while today is an end unlike anything we've ever seen, somehow some part of us will survive this, too, and our joys and sorrows will endure, perhaps in the eternal memory of God. I guess now I feel a kind of blessed calm, that this end, no less than the others the Jewish people have known, is intended by

God." And after she says this, for a second the sun seems brighter than it has ever been. Even in the shadow of the house, three generations can feel its new intensity.

After the air is done echoing the weight of what the mother has said, the sort of hope that makes the light brighter, she asks, "What do you think of all this?" The young man replies, "Isn't that an impossible question: What do I think of all that?" She responds by saying, "Sure, but still," to which he says, "What do you want, a rant?" She says, "If that is what's needed, I will listen." The young man is growing angry although he is not exactly sure why, but he knows it is not his mother's fault. Today is the end of the world, and there is no part of him that wants to spend it being mean to his mother. He tries to take a deep breath before he responds. Focusing on doing that, he falls off the beams and starts his balancing again. He takes a couple of deep breaths and starts talking:

"I guess I just don't even know where to begin, because if I really think about what I'm feeling, it's just too much to hold, too much to say... I'm terrified and traumatized, and at the same time, so fucking angry. And, look, I'm sorry to curse, and I'm sorry to be angry, but I want to be able to be honest with you, and I want to show you that I'm trying hard for the sake of our family to be okay. But I'm not okay. I mean, you got to live your life. Sure, you want to keep on living, and I'm sorry that you won't get to live to be as old as Zayde, but I'm just starting my life. I feel like I just became self-aware like five years ago or less, and now my life's over. Everything is over. I'm so angry at everybody who's come before me—even if I'm carrying them in my bones, right now I don't feel proud... I mean, maybe there could have been a way to stop what is happening tonight if we could have focused on working together and treating each other with dignity—Hell, we ruined the world long before tonight. And yeah, our people have been killed in so many ways, but so have so many other kinds of people. People have been evil and wicked to each other forever, and it sucks, and it's so unfair. Where are the righteous? Where have they ever been? I've been keeping a journal since the Announcement, and I thought it could be a Tzadik type of experience to write down my life, to try to justify all this, us and our lives and the end, I guess, to God or at least to myself. And I have been reading what I wrote all day, and I just keep coming back to this question: Where is God? Where was he then, and where is he now? I want so much to believe in him. I want to live righteously like a Tzadik. I want the writing I've done to show him that there is something worth saving down here. But where is he? Where was he in Auschwitz? Where was he when they burned down Zayde's hometown, our hometown, that we'll never get to go back to and wouldn't have anyway even if all this shit hadn't happened? Where was he during slavery and colonialism and every other atrocity? Where is his plan? If all this is part of it, I can't believe. I want to. Look, I really want to, and I have tried so hard to. I have spent so much of my time this month trying to will myself to have a moment of belief, to see the sunlight as a sign from above that everything is going to be okay, but the sun is nothing but a burning thing a hundred million miles away. Some moments—before all this—I could almost believe in God. I almost could, but with all this, I just don't know how. I thought through writing all this down, through trying to keep track of my life and all we have lost, that it might make sense, but I'm not even sure what making sense means, or if it's even possible at all. I want to be like the Tzadiks. I want to think that we're a chosen people, that we've survived for so long for a reason. I want there to be a reason more than anything. I want there to be a reason, and I sit in my room, and I look at the light and jot down moments I want to remember from my life, and I wait for a miracle, and I wait for a sign. I want there to be something bigger than all this, than us. I want to make you proud by being good and righteous and live as if at any moment I could realize I'm made to live as an example of humanity in the eyes of God. But I don't know how to do it. I'm not just. I'm not brave. I'm terrified, and my girlfriend is gone, and I have no idea if she ever even made it home, and my sister is God knows where and…"

His speech trails off here; he lacks the energy to keep going. The young man grows quiet and stands with his hands over his face and his body slightly shaking. His mother puts out what must have been her fourth or fifth cigarette in a row, stands up, and gives him a hug. "I'm sorry," she says. "Me too," says her son, even though none of this is anyone's fault. They stand in an embrace until it gets too hot to do so, and then his mother goes inside. He can tell she is going to cry and doesn't want to do it in front of him. He realizes, then, that this must be twice as hard for her as it is for him, because while her life is ending, both the lives she helped create are ending too.

The young man goes inside now too, feeling drained from all that has just been said and heard and felt. The day is nearly halfway done.

1

While living with three other young men and the seemingly endless line of people cycling through his rental house—and bathroom and shower—it was disgusting for the young man to even imagine taking a bath, though he often wanted to. But here, in his parents' house, there are two bathtubs, which are kept clean, and to which his father rigged the plumbing so that water can come out near boiling. The young man's father likes to take baths so hot that in winter the windows in the whole house fog up.

For the past month, the young man has been bathing in the late afternoons during the hottest part of the July day. There is no air conditioning in the house because the father refused to install it. His opinions regarding air conditioning are expressed in such phrases as: "AC is a goddamn waste," "Summertime is made for sweatin'," and "If y'all want to be cool in the summer, y'all can get a job in the freezer department of the grocery store down the road, stockin' shelves while I enjoy the warmth while it's around." The father said the last one so much when the children were growing up that they both got jobs at the grocery store at different times in their high school careers. There, they wore puffy coats and gloves throughout the summer while their friends worked as lifeguards or camp counselors. After working that job, they never complained about the air conditioning or lack thereof again and learned to deal with the heat in their own ways. Baths at midday are how the young man has learned to survive the summer, after growing up in the unmitigated heat invading through the windows and open doors. With a bath in the middle of the day, he can make himself feel hotter than it ever is outside, so that when he gets out, he feels cool for the rest of the day.

After the talk with his mother on the patio, and the subsequent rush of feeling that came with finally speaking his mind after so long, the young man goes into the bathroom and takes off his clothes. Before he starts the water, in the blue-grey brightness of the glossed window, using first scissors and then an industrial-strength electric razor, he cuts the hair from his neck and cheeks and chin and head. He moves the razor slowly from his forehead back to the nape of his neck, leaving pale flesh where there were coarse curls seconds before. Hair loops softly through the air and onto the sink. After ten minutes with those tools of removal in his hands, the young man's face is smooth, and his head is fuzzy in a way which he knows his girlfriend would have loved to caress. He gathers what once grew from inside of him and out through him into the world, drops it in the basin of the toilet, and flushes it away. Naked in front of the mirror, he gives himself a nod with a fresh face then takes a bath so hot his eyes throb.

1

After the bath, the young man wraps himself in a towel, selects a track to play on a record, removes the towel from his body, lays it down on the floor, and lies down on it, his body coffined in the afternoon light coming through the window in grey oblong shafts that pattern the floor in rounded shapes and flicker with the wind outside. The song he plays is "Casimir Pulaski Day" by Sufjan Stevens. He loves this song because it is about faith and love and the small details that make people who they are. He listens to Stevens sing about a friend who has cancer, how they pray over her body, but no matter the prayers, her condition does not change. With this song and the sun all around, the young man thinks about all the unanswered prayers, about the almighty silence that has fallen over the world. But as he listens, he wonders if silence is really just silence, or if it is actually an answer of some kind—maybe it is a louder answer than anything that could ever be spoken. An answer he didn't particularly want to receive. An answer that makes him shiver. To distract himself from the silence, the divine response that abounds everywhere, he opens his notebook to a section he wrote after a bath like the one he just took.

11

At certain times, like when I'm sitting at my desk in my room and light streams in from outdoors, a feeling comes over me, a feeling that's not completely unlike thinking—perhaps it's the feeling of getting lost in thought? A stillness comes, and for a moment my mind is still. But there's more to it than that. I'm out of my body for several seconds—if time isn't completely lost—and nothing registers in memory. Then suddenly I return. I return, but it's as if I've been right there the whole time, just unmoving and slightly off center of myself, a spirit barely lifted from a bodily form.

I can't control when this experience will come over me at my desk, but I can actively seek it while taking a bath. It's a precious away-ness where I no longer have the burden of thought, yet I'm mysteriously still conscious. Since the Announcement, I've been trying to get out of my head in this way, because the more I think about the end, the worse and more real it gets. If I take a bath as hot as I can possibly stand, like I did today, things will start to happen. I put my head under the water, closing my nose with pinched fingers. Soon, in the heat and rippling water, my very being seems to become a vibration and my heart a cannon in my core and I focus on this as I hold my breath. My body throbs, and for a second the mass of it lifts and I'm floating and I'm free. In these moments, or maybe right after, I hope that this is what death will feel like, just a soft separation up into the sky.

But when I get out, standing barefoot on the cool tile floor, and the sky outside is blazing, and everything seems unflawed and young, it's only a matter of time before I begin to remember what I've been trying so hard to forget. I remember it and feel the weight again on my shoulders and on my back, and there's nothing I want to do more than forget again, even for a moment, what I'm facing, what my family—the whole world—is facing.

1

Earlier, as the family stood in the kitchen eating ice cream and trying not to lose their minds, the mother asked if everybody would write some letters, which she wanted them to burn. She said the family should write to the people they love who weren't there to hear their final goodbyes, that maybe through the writing and the subsequent conversion to ash through the catalyst of flame, they could somehow get these farewells out and into the air. She said that maybe through the fire the energy of what was written could be released. And though the young man isn't sure he believes in the energy or the ability to send messages to those he loves through grey flecks in the sky and wind, he figures having something to toss into the flames could be a good start to the end of everything.

After lying on the floor of his room while his body readjusted to its full weight, he steps back into the bathroom to hang the towel, and in the mirror his face and hair are so changed, he is unrecognizable and small. His cheeks look empty and so do his eyes. He is sweating with the residual heat of the steam and rush of the bath. He opens the window to let in some fresh air, and with that air comes the sound of the dog, which rings off the walls. He returns to his room, sits down at the desk, and begins to write.

First he wants to write something to his sister. He sits there for many minutes in the sun through the window, sweating, unable to get anything worthwhile out. He misses her and is so angry at her for not being there and mostly he hopes that somewhere she is ok. Yet, all this emotion somehow does not translate to any meaningful scratches on the page, just screams in gel pen black which help him in no way. He crumples up a barely scribbled-on sheet from his notebook, tosses it in the trash and tries to move on. He starts on something to his girlfriend. In ink on plain white paper, he puts down his best attempt at describing his love and what it meant to lose it.

He tries and tries, and unlike the past month—when words flowed like water from a broken faucet onto the pages of his pink unicorn notebook—now he can't seem to say anything. He starts page after page in the notebook, beginning with "Dear" and "Hello" or simply her name, but there is nothing that follows, like the nothing that follows everything after today, and he ends up with fifteen torn out and balled up pages on the desk and nothing written at all—the emotion can only be expressed in the silence of those crumpled balls of lined paper, a silence louder and more real than anything he could have written anyway. So he will burn this silence, for at least this silence he can do something about, and he turns back to his writing from ten days before, to quell the burning he feels in his gut for having tried and failed to write something worthwhile today, to try to find something else to move toward and into besides the silence that is starting to hurt his head.

10

I'm a lot like my mom. People often say we have the same blue eyes, the same mouth and wide nose, and the same overwhelming emotional responses to everyday things. We are so similar that we have, at times, a near telepathic bond. Although I was raised to see myself in my mom, in the last two years, I have started to try and see the ways I'm like my dad too. I was feeling distant from him and wanted to understand what we had in common so we could grow closer. After all, my dad is as much a part of me as my mom is—or, as my dad says, I'm "the sum of our parts," after which he always winks. I figured, by learning about and from my dad, I could learn more about myself, and in turn feel better about my relationship with the man who helped bring me into the world.

I mainly see my dad in myself in the sounds I make when I sit down or the appearance of my face in the mirror when I brush my teeth or comb back my hair. And after a couple years of trying to get to know my dad as an adult, I have learned that we have our taste and passion for music in common as well.

For as long as I can remember, I've loved folk music, by which I mean American folk music. The folk music of the Jews of Eastern Europe that Zayde sometimes listens to, never really became part of my musical taste. Sometimes I think my mom has wondered about this, perhaps even regretted it, but the fact remains that Jewish traditional music seems no more like a living thing to me than Yiddish, which, after all, my mom never taught me. It was my dad who showed me the music I love the most, and he began doing so when my sister and I were young. He would drive us to school in his truck, blasting Neil Young or The Indigo Girls and singing along, open-mouthed and out of key.

After all that has happened, all the questions about how to live a good life in the waning days of everything, I figure the least I can do is make sure to spend as many intentional moments as possible with each person in my family, to watch the time pass on others' faces instead of through the sun on the walls. And I know that in the last of the light and the last of the dark too, the time I spend with my dad must involve music.

1

Inspired by his own words, the young man walks down the hall to the room in which he will find his father. When the house was built, the room was meant to be a large walk-in closet, but now it is a place where his father often sits half-naked listening to records and smoking cigarettes and where his mother writes. His parents store their books and elk antlers and whatever else in the room the young man is staying in now, but they work and spend time in this makeshift office across the hall from where the grandfather sleeps, and dances at night when he thinks nobody is awake to hear.

In one corner of this office, there is an old wooden desk on which there is only a stack of lined paper and three black ballpoint pens. This is where the young man's mother has handwritten the first drafts of her three published books and countless other unpublished pieces which will now never see the light outside of the file cabinet. Some of the young man's earliest memories are of sitting in this office beside his mother's desk while she hummed and wrote, chewing on pen caps as she filled blue lines with black ink.

In the corner opposite his mother's mostly empty desk is a brown corduroy recliner and a bookshelf filled with records. On top of the bookshelf sits a record player with external speakers and a headphone jack with a splitter for when two people want to listen to a record at once. The young man's father bought the recliner for seven dollars at a thrift store in 1983 and has schlepped it from house to house for years. He has told the young man on more than one occasion, and the mother has confirmed this with a roll of her eyes, that one of the best things about buying a house was that he didn't have to move the chair around anymore. Because it has been moved so much, was beaten up when the father bought it, and is used almost every day, the thing is faded and ripped and creaky and falling apart, but the father loves it almost as much as he loves his family, or so he sometimes jokes. When the family teases about throwing it out, the father gets a quiet sort of mad and sits in the chair in protest.

The father has almost as many nicknames for the chair as he does for everything else, one of which is his *other special lady*. He will sit in his other special lady most days after work, and in this chair the father will undergo what he calls *the cool down*, which proceeds as follows. First, he takes a bath. Then, he puts on a pair of jeans and goes into the office. He leans the chair back, and when the foot support pops out, he stretches his long legs to the edge. He cracks the window behind the chair so *Mama*—which is, even now, still a name for the young man's mother—doesn't get mad about the smoke he is about to soak the room in. Then he lights what he calls a *puffer* and puts on a record and a pair of noise-canceling headphones. He then listens to a whole record straight through, his eyes closed, exhaling smoke out of his slightly crooked, forever sightly-sunburned nose.

The father has told the young man as many times as he has told him everything else that no matter how long or gruesome each workday is, sitting in the chair and going through the cool down solves it all. No matter if the father was "diggin'" or "sittin' in the excavator" or "in some crawl space fightin' off rats," once he can have a seat and rest for the time it takes to play a record, he will be refreshed—reborn, even. For this reason, the father also calls the chair his *corduroy fountain of youth*. As he tells it, after about an hour in those brown and sunbeaten folds, "I come out the other side of the record a new freakin' man." He says he has blown away so many bad days with smoke and sound, going through half a pack of cigarettes, tapping them into the ashtray he places on his stomach while reclined, his legs crossed at the ankles at the edge of the foot rest. In the chair, one can see the indentation of years, the weight of the father making a faint shape of his body over time, slightly darker than the rest of the chair, an echo of so many afternoons spent with his eyes closed.

The young man's father does all this after a bath, and so the young man supposes that his love of baths is something else he inherited from his father. His baths, his small movements, his music: this is the young man's paternal inheritance. His father knows more about folk music, old country, and folk rock than anybody the young man has ever met. Even though the father is nearing sixty, the young man still goes to him when he wants new music. Before the Announcement, his father often emailed or texted or called him about new songs he heard on the radio through a jobsite boombox he always took to work. And so today, after his bath and after being reminded by his own reflections of his connection to his father through the music they have shared, the young man strides down the hall, hoping to listen to some songs with him, to share those sounds sunk in vinyl and played through a needle straight into both of their hearts.

1

Many people, at certain times in life, think of their parents as superheroes, and a part of the young man has never let go of that picture of his father. On some level, the young man hopes when he comes upon his father this afternoon, that the man will have miraculously solved the situation they are all in. While the young man knows what he is thinking is ridiculous, he walks down the hall wide-eyed and full of hope for the first time in a month. He turns the corner into the office and sees his father on the floor. The father is kneeling, shirtless and weeping, his shoulder blades made into long lines of sharp bone pressing tightly against the skin of his back. His whole body heaves with each sob-fractured breath. The shadow he casts on the hardwood, made possible by the crisp, plastery light, is skinny and small. He is not making much sound, trying to keep what is going on to himself.

The young man has seen his father cry before, but not like this. He has never seen anyone cry like this. His father looks so tiny, so shattered, crazed with sorrow. The young man wants to go to his father and put a hand on his shoulder. But the father hasn't seen him yet, and the young man somehow knows seeing his father see him would ruin the moment of communion between them that he had hoped for. There are some truths that should never be faced, some facts and failures that are nobody's fault, and which only do harm to discuss. The young man realizes, and his whole body understands, in this moment, that his father cannot save them, that nobody can, and this knowing feels like a heavy rock in his gut. There are no superheroes. They have never existed, and soon, neither will anything else. He understands this now more than he ever has.

The young man backs out of the doorway as quietly as possible and retraces his steps back down the hall. Then he walks much more loudly toward the door to the room his father is in, clearing his throat and slightly stomping his feet. When he knocks on the threshold of the office door and makes eye contact with his father, the father nods at the young man like the whole world is fine. There is nothing to be said about what the young man just saw, so he takes a breath and pretends everything is okay. Closing the door behind him, he goes and sits on the floor beside his father's recliner. His father, despite his slightly puffy eyes, is fresh out of his daily bath, which he took right after the young man was finished. The father installed a second water heater a few years back, so nobody ever had to take a cold bath. The father's grey-blonde hair is shoulder-length and wet and has been slicked back with a comb. He is wearing faded and work-worn blue jeans with a hole in the left knee and neither shirt nor socks. He appears to be in good shape, better shape than the young man has ever been in, no matter how much the young man has worked out. The only part of his father's body that shows his age are his feet, which are callused and long-toed.

The father has his headphones in his hand and is about to put them on. A cigarette, unlit, hangs from his thin lips. A record is on the turntable, ready to spin and make music with the push of a button. The father says nothing to his son as he lights his cigarette with a gold-plated Zippo adorned with an engraving of a backhoe that one of his friends got him when his excavation company turned twenty. The father blows the first puff of smoke straight up, apparently forgetting or maybe not caring about the window he opened to blow smoke out of. The light in the room, somehow less harsh now that the father isn't sobbing on the floor, shines around the smoke, making it glimmer. There's a cord and an extra pair of noise-canceling headphones on the bottom shelf where the records are kept. Usually, the mother uses these headphones, but now the father hands them to his son after flicking some ash into the clear glass ashtray on the arm of the chair. The young man takes the headphones and puts them on, feeling like a kid wearing an oversized helmet. The father looks at his son then leans down and gives the young man's freshly shaven head a rub. The young man laughs, shirks away from his father's hand, and gives him a thumbs-up. The father's eyes are red from crying, yet there is also a joyous glint that the son is happy to see: there is a light in his father that has not gone out, a miracle like the flame of the Maccabees persists, a glimmer in the dark.

There is no sound yet, just the whoosh the record makes before the needle hits. The father sits down in the chair, creaks open the fold-out foot rest, leans back, and sets the ashtray on his bare chest. He takes a big puff of his cigarette, twists toward the window, and blows the smoke through his nose and mouth at the same time, watching for a moment as the pressure of the open window sucks the smoke out and swirls it away. The young man closes his eyes and relaxes his body against the white wall. The drywall is cool against his freshly shaved head. The music begins.

They are listening to one of the father's most recent favorite albums, Charlie Parr's *Stumpjumper*. He introduced his son to the album one day while the young man was helping at one of his father's jobsites. They listened to the album over and over on a battery-powered boombox as they moved a massive pile of gravel with shovels and a wheelbarrow up a hill too steep and forested for the backhoe to access. Since that day in the sun, the young man has listened to this album many times, and it has become one of his favorites as well. His father likes it so much he had to buy a new copy of the record, because he warped it from overuse. He was proud that, by simply listening to something, he had been able to make it change its shape. He said to his son that "It was like some sorta magic, movin' matter with my mind." The young man doesn't know if it is was magic or an unhealthy obsession that warped the old record, but both of them can agree that the best song on the album is "Over the Red Cedar." The profound lyrics of this song, which the young man deeply resonated with when he first heard them and which still move him now, speak of Tuesday afternoons and how they seem to defy time with their length, and how over the years, even these work days, which once seemed endless, become something one misses as their life passes by. Parr describes how time always moves on and there is no reclaiming it once it's gone.

And today is a Tuesday which, like so many others, the young man wants to end and to go on forever at once. And although he knows it is impossible to imagine himself missing something after the world ends, after everything, including himself, is reduced to nothing, he still thinks of things he will miss. Perhaps it is more a feeling than a thought, and that is why it does not matter that it makes no sense. He will miss how, for three minutes, a good song can take him away from whatever else is going on. Away from time and the countdown— or the buildup—to the final minute. Away from questions about God. Away from missing his lost love. Away from thoughts of a sister who never came home. Away from the questions about if he will spend his final time in the best, most just and useful way. The young man will miss time itself: the too much and too little of it that used to define life. He will miss the way it dragged at work, the way three to five in the afternoon seemed to stretch a full day's length, the way this past month has seemed like both a lifetime and less than a day. While he is beside his father, he would give anything for the minutes to slow down. He wants time to stand still, to live forever at that almost three o'clock, as the song he is now listening to so poetically puts it. He must stay present and make use of what little time he has left. The young man watches his father, his eyes closed, lift his cigarettes to his lips, inhale, exhale, sigh, and tap the ash into the ashtray. The light is soft, and the smoke veils the bright world outside. With one hand, the father holds his cigarette between two extended fingers, and with the other, he keeps time on his skin by drumming his fingers, making the ashtray on his torso wobble in time with the slide and strum of the guitar. The young man reaches his hand up and puts it on his father's shoulder, and they sit together like that, time moving as fast as it always has, as the record, and everything else, spins toward silence.

1

As the last sounds of the last song on the record fade, the mother calls the family out to the back yard, and the father and the son follow the call. The whole family stands there squinting on the sun-flattened grass. The heat of the day is made visible in waves which rise from the flagstone of the patio. The plants in the garden and yard are wilted and lack the sheen they had in the cool and shade of morning. At this time of year, the sun sets around twenty minutes after nine and rises around six, which means there is sunlight on the back yard for more than fifteen hours a day. The whole world is being baked, and the way the plants look in the middle of the day is proof. Under the hammering sun and the weight of his body, the cowlicked tufts of lawn beneath the young man's feet are jagged and brown, hardened like something pulled too late from an oven.

The father fires up a metal trash can by squirting lighter fluid onto a pile of crunched-up papers. At first, the young man thinks his father is burning newspaper or scraps of paper, but he looks closer and realizes that the blackened papers are birth certificates and financial documents like the title to the house and the trucks in the driveway. The young man thinks he even saw a stack of hundred-dollar bills in the can. He raises his eyebrows and his father shrugs, saying "Ain't good for nothin' but fire now." The young man supposes that can be said about everything else, too.

Each family member has their letters with them, their hands clutch inky-paper soon to wane into windborne, fluttering grey. Everybody seems to be readying themselves for this goodbye. They are quiet and looking down like they are trying not to cry, with the exception of the grandfather, who smokes a cigarette and sips a can of grape soda loudly between puffs, as if there were endless time and no worry in the world.

They are all sweating and standing in a misshapen circle around the quickly blackening metal can. The air smells of trash fire, a dark, smoky thing that hits the back of their throats and makes their eyes water if they stand too close. The father grows impatient at the growth of the fire and squirts about half a bottle of lighter fluid into the can, lights a match on his thumbnail, and tosses it dramatically into the fire like an action movie hero. The new flames make the many gold teeth in his smile glint. As the family stands, watching the father enjoy himself a little bit too much, the wind is thin and hot on their necks. The smell of lighter fluid and burning paper is on the air. The light of the afternoon, outside of the spinning plume of blue-black smoke coming from the trash can, is rose gold.

The young man's girlfriend often talked about how this song or that song would be playing at certain points in their lives if their lives were a movie, and in line with the common side effects of the contagions of love and proximity, his mind adopted the patterns of his girlfriend and he too started to try to find the soundtrack of his day-to-day living. As the family stands around the fire, the young man thinks about what music would play now. He decides that it would be "La Dispute" by the pianist Yann Tiersen. When Tiersen was young and alone, living in a rented house by the sea, he was captivated by a lighthouse and wrote an album in honor of it as well as his seclusion. The young man has long since loved stories of people braving solitude and despair to create grand pieces of art. Though perhaps he doesn't realize it, he has always fancied himself as this sort of person, one who could face the void and come back with something worth showing the world. But the urge to go into vast wilds alone stands in contradiction to the binds of his family and his girlfriend. This past month has been the closest he has come to sitting alone in despair with the chance to make something of it. He has not had—and he will not have—the time to reconcile the competing calls of community and solitude, to live out both truths—that of his time making his mark on the world and that of his time with his girlfriend making breakfast on slow mornings in fall. He will not have time to understand how these two things are in fact one. And yet Tiersen's songs, like all art, will persist, signifying and symbolizing as they always have: a symptom of holy accident, that hidden righteousness when one finds oneself in a place where all has failed, yet something beautiful emerges.

The young man went to New York last year with his girlfriend, and on one of the days they were there, they went to Ellis Island, where so many of the young man's family first set foot in America. As soon as the young man stepped off the ferry and onto that speck of Earth where the people who made him had passed through all those years ago, he felt the many hands of history pulling at him. There, where so many Jews were made safe, in the heart of that beacon of the New World, he knew that day was going to be more than a simple visit to a museum. This was a chance to walk the path of his ancestors, to feel what they felt, to travel if only for an afternoon backward in time. Telling his girlfriend he needed some time on his own, he put on his headphones, played "La Dispute" on repeat, and then traced the steps taken by his family two generations before he was born. There was something in the music that matched the flat-mouthed faces of those who fied across the sea, blown up into massive portraits and hung on the walls. The sun through the wide, high windows unraveled onto a tile where so many millions of weary feet passed through, illuminating the great choice: Leave the only small place in the world you know for a dream of something better or stay home and die—the very choice his ancestors made that placed him here, and would eventually allow his family to stand in the back yard of a fortified suburban home, burning letters on the last day of the world. But today, instead of music, they have quiet, broken only by the barking of the dog down the street and the burning crackle of legal documents, money, and all the other papers that used to define their lives.

The young man steps toward the quickly darkening metal first. He doesn't say anything, because he feels that if he did, he would spend the rest of the day talking, trying to figure out a perfect introduction to the last words he has not been able to write. He simply tosses the crumpled-up pages of the unfinished letters into the trash can, and for a second the flames rise high and red before puffing out some ash and black smoke and then sinking back beneath the circle of steel.

As he watches the empty paper turn to nothing but a stain on the air, he remembers all the words his girlfriend wrote to him on sticky notes over the past two years, and he runs inside to his room. There he finds the wooden box and brings it out into the day. Stepping over the extinguisher and the pitcher of water on the stoop outside the door that his father set there just in case, he moves onto the dry grass. He opens the wooden box and holds it upside down. Sticky notes like autumn leaves flitter through the air above the fire. Overcome with the moment, he doesn't think about the wind and the distance between his hands and the trash can. About twenty of the several hundred hand-written notes scatter in the wind before they can be eaten up by the reaching flames, blowing across the yard and over the fence. Realizing he may lose more notes to the air, the young man asks his father for the lighter fluid, douses the box and what is left of the paper and tosses it all into the fire. A small explosion ensues, and the family collectively takes a big step back. Soon the flames retreat.

The father's writing is on a yellow legal pad which he used to use for estimates and landscape designs for customers. Instead of stepping forward to speak, the father stands beside his wife at the edge of the circle and mumbles his hopes that his buddies from work are "doin' ok" and how he wishes he "coulda had a few beers with each and every one of 'em before, well, before today." As he speaks, he crumples the pages and tosses them into the trash can basketball-style. He makes the first three into the can, but on the fourth and final page, he misses. The paper passes through the fire, goes up in smoke, and lands on the side of the trash can opposite him. There, the paper and the section of lawn beneath it start to burn. The father jogs over and puts everything out with his boot, then dumps the pitcher of water onto the lawn and sprays the now-wet-and-black spot with the extinguisher for good measure. As he puts out the small fire, which the young man is beginning to think his father may have started just for the sake of being able to use the fire extinguisher, the father laughs softly and says, "Glad I got that fire out, 'cause I don't want to go and kill us before we all die."

Tucked under her arm, the mother holds a stack of at least thirty envelopes, addressed and stamped and sealed. She's even taken the time to put the family's return address on the left front corner of each envelope in her loopy cursive. She lists the names of the dozens of people she wrote to, including her daughter. She holds that envelope in her hand and gaze longer than any other. As she lists the names, they are interrupted by the breaking of her voice as it is made hoarse by her tears. Before she drops all she has in the fire, she gives a speech that sounds almost like a sermon, and her voice breaks no longer, like there is something else there within her, helping her to say what she needs to.

"Tomorrow, if it were to come, would be Tisha B'av, a day of remembering the Temple that was burned, not once, but twice. On that day, I would fast and I would try to refrain from smiling or laughing. I would try to refrain from chatting idly. I would try to be somber and remember the rain of ashes and all that we have lost over and over, yet I would also remember that we remain, that somehow we have remained. I believe that, like the Temple, some semblance of us will remain after tonight, the same semblance in us that has survived all that we have, all the thousands of years of exile, all the deserts and encampments and smoking ruins. And today these letters are my own temple, the temple of my heart, and they will burn like so much has, like so many of us have burned, like we may tonight. But I'm not afraid of the fire anymore, and I'll smile and laugh and chat idly today, for I know that there is more beyond the flames, that there always has been."

She then steps forward and releases the stack of paper and ink. At first, her letters almost kill the fire, but then the trash can erupts with flames, blue-green, then yellow, then the orange of the purest sun and of the very heart of the world.

The grandfather sways back and forth during most of the family's ceremony. He shifts his weight side to side and keeps his eyes down, a lit American Spirit in his mouth and a can of grape soda in one of his ever-so-slightly shaking hands. When everybody has said their piece, burned what they needed to burn, let go of whom and what they could, the young man figures they will watch the fire burn itself out and then go inside. Nobody expects the grandfather to really know what is going on, and certainly not to participate, but once everybody has taken a turn, he steps toward the flames. He finishes his can of soda, tosses it and the tiny bit left of his cigarette into the flames, and pulls a dog-eared, rubber-band-bound notebook from inside his cardigan. With the flair for the dramatic that both the young man and the mother seem to have inherited, he then takes out another cigarette, bends down, and lights it in the reeking flames.

He leans back, looking up at the sky, draws a long breath and exhales through his nose, then opens the notebook. It is full of pencil drawings of the family, so finely detailed they look like black-and-white photographs. He pages through maybe a hundred images over the next few minutes, holding the notebook flat so the family can see what is on each page. The only sound is the crackling of the fire, the yipping of the dog down the street, and the occasional flipping of paper. There is a drawing of the young man on the patio in a white t-shirt and jeans, looking up at the stars, his arms and chest generously muscular, his face sullen and bearded, his hair curly and near shoulder-length, like some modern rabbi looking up beyond the sky for answers from above.

Another of the old man's drawings is of the father and the mother dancing in the office, framed through a half-open door. Another is of the young man's garden, the plants as detailed as if the drawing came from the hand of a botanist, the flowers seeming to shine with life on the page even without color. The grandfather has captured so many little moments, things that are sacred because they were most likely the last time the family would do these things. The young man sees his grandfather now as a Tzadik, a righteous one with a pencil and a houseful of miracles to transcribe.

The family protests with groans as the patriarch moves toward the fire, but as he holds his notebook high above his head, the family stands still and silent. Even the dog down the street makes no sound for the seconds it takes the pages to fall in slow motion through the smoke-choked air. The pages make the fire turn momentarily green. All these moments of the family's lives at first char, then kill the flame. The dog starts barking again. The air is stagnant and opaque and heavy. After the father empties the rest of the fire extinguisher onto the trash can for good measure, the family filters through the soot and sun back into the house.

After coming inside from the ceremony and changing his clothes, which stink of sweat and trash fire, the young man sits at his desk, puts on his headphones, and plays a record he has listened to nearly every day since he has returned to his parents' house—the very album he will momentarily read about in his own words. The music links him to who he was then, to what he was, to where he was—all of seven days ago, seven days which he would give anything to have again.

7

I'm sitting here at my desk with one week left to live, listening to the album *In the Aeroplane Over the Sea* by Neutral Milk Hotel. I love this album at least in part because the lead singer, Jeff Mangum, was inspired to write these songs because of the story of Anne Frank. Every time I think about her, I think how if Zayde hadn't come to America when he did, fleeing the growing shadow of the Third Reich, part of my family would've had to hide and would eventually have been killed like she was.

In the last twenty-three days, I've listened to this record over and over while thinking about Anne Frank. I think of how I'm hiding out with my family in this house. I know my experience isn't the same as what she went through, but I feel a warm resonance with it, some similar vibration weaving through the decades. She was facing her end, trying to make sense of and live her life through writing, while still trying to spend time with her family, and trying to understand a God she was learning to believe in in her own way. I think that maybe the story of my last days is something bigger than me, twisting back in time to meet the other ends of the world, from Anne Frank's to that of Zayde's hometown to those of the Tzadiks. And in the story that we've all tried to tell, the sense we've tried to make of the world and of God and of what lies beyond life, we are and forever will be together.

"Oh, Comely," plays through my headphones now, in which Mangum sings about how he wishes he had a time machine so he could go back and save all the people who were killed so brutally, all the families and children robbed of all things precious to them: time, love, life. It's been about eighty years since the end of the world for so many Jews, in the camps or the burnt shtetls like the one where Zayde was born and which was wiped away in the war. For so many, long before today, the end of the world came—for those dragged here in the bottoms of boats or forced by violence to the fringes of this so-called New World. And sure, the end of the world is coming, but the more I think about it, the more I realize the end has already happened so many times.

Later in the album is the song "Two Headed Boy, Pt. 2." which I sit listening to now in the dimness of my seventh-to-last day of life. There's a line in this song that's been on my mind a lot this month. It details a view of God not as a thing, but a place, a site of something gorgeous and holy and good. When I hear this now, something clicks within me, and even though I'm not sure if I've ever really believed in God, I begin to hope there is something beyond these seven days. I hope there is some great place where everyone goes upon dying. Some field of endless, soft green or a beach of white sand, bordered by the crashing of clear, perfect water. I feel a solace knowing so many endings have come before, and I can't help but feel this solace is an intuition that there is something beyond the end, that God was not just a story people told themselves, a hopeful lie they were able to believe, for a while at least.

1

After finishing the album, the young man goes into the kitchen to make dinner, which is going to be shell pasta with ground elk bolognese. He and his girlfriend found the recipe for this particular sauce scribbled in the margins of the 18th edition of *The Complete Dog Book*, which they bought at a yard sale last year for one dollar. They had been trying to cook more in order to save money but had never known what to cook and took the discovery of the recipe in this random book as a sign to get started. They made bolognese the same night.

In an effort to make use of himself and give something like thanks to his family, the young man wants to share this recipe by making it for them. He has never cooked for them before and is nervous he is going to ruin their last dinner. He hopes to make this last gathering at the kitchen table special, this last circle of chairs, one of them empty—as if for Elijah, at the Passover Seder—though in this family it is reserved for the missing sister and daughter who would make the family whole.

For his sauce, he uses meat from an animal his father shot and vegetables that the young man grew himself: something killed by the man who gave him life, mixed with something he helped bring into being. He starts by getting out the biggest saucepot he can find in his parents' cabinets. Thirty years of meals and memories are contained within this pot. With this meal, the young man hopes to bring forth the sense of family that has been boiled into the metal.

While the young man cooks, the grandfather sits on a stool by the refrigerator. The grandfather is in the young man's way, and he is a little bit annoyed that he has to work around him. When the young man thinks about trying to describe, in their broken way of communicating, how he needs his grandfather to move, he looks at this man—the reason he is alive, this man who made that great flight across the sea, who is so small in his chair though his eyes are big and loving—and there is no way the young man can tell him to move. The young man realizes then that he would choose to have his grandfather there, in his way, rather than not have him there at all.

As the young man cuts vegetables and moves back and forth between the refrigerator and the sink and the trash can, the grandfather starts speaking. Although the young man has no idea what his grandfather is saying, his words seem passionate. His brow is furrowed and he moves his hands wildly as he speaks and there are a lot of *Jesus Christ*s—for emphasis, perhaps. The young man works around him and nods as if he knows exactly what is being said.

He first cooks three white onions from his garden, the only onions he was able to grow this year and which he has been saving for a special occasion. They are fist-sized, and he cubes them after peeling back the outer layers of flaky skin. While he is cutting them, his eyes start to water *somethin' fierce*, as his father would say. He stumbles bleary-eyed toward the sink, tears streaming down his face, his nose running, his hands held out. He is so distracted by the stinging blindness that he forgets about his grandfather and the stool and runs into them. The grandfather stands up quickly, mumbling "nope, nope, nope" under his breath, and pulls his grandson into a tight hug.

The young man's hands are sticky with onion juice and at first he isn't crying, just reacting to the airborne onion spray. He stands limp in the old man's surprisingly strong arms, waiting for the hug to be over, trying not to get any snot or tears or bits of cut-up vegetables on the grandfather's threadbare cardigan, which is scratchy against the skin of the young man's arms. The old man smells like cigarettes and old soap, the white bar kind with a clean, chemical smell. His grandfather's scent overwhelms the young man as he takes a deep breath, trying to figure out how to tell his grandfather that he is not really crying, all while the grandfather holds his grandson in a hug, mumbling in Yiddish, occasionally saying things the young man can understand like "atta boy."

The young man looks over his grandfather's shoulder as they remain in the embrace, the grandfather still mumbling to himself or maybe to the young man. The young man can see down his grandfather's back, and he sees that his cardigan is tucked into his underwear. He can see his grandfather's faded briefs, thin and frayed with age. This is what makes the young man start to cry for real, and he pulls his grandfather tight into the hug, deciding that his grandfather won't mind the schmutz on his grandson's hands. What breaks the young man's heart in this moment is how hard his grandfather was trying to keep things together, how close he was to doing so, how close they all were to being okay. He has turned the right shoulder of his grandfather's cardigan from green to wet black with his tears. The young man thinks how his girlfriend would have called this scene tragicute.

The young man has no idea if his grandfather knows what today is, what the weight of every moment holds, but no matter what he does or does not know, the young man understands that his grandfather is still trying to get up and straighten his hat and tuck in his shirt each day. Today, he was so close to getting it right. Yes, this is what does the young man in, how it is all nearly alright, the whole world: the way, if you look, everything seems fine at first, but if you look closer, you notice the seams that split, the paint that peels, the rancid smell on the wind, a stain on the shirt you thought was clean, all the small rot and the winding down of the hours.

The young man is lost in the warmth of the embrace of this man whom he has never been able to understand, this man who lost the ability to communicate with his grandson at the same time his grandson gained the desire to engage with his elder. This is the man who brought the family here in his body across so much water and light, the man who worked himself mad so that his descendants could have a good life—until this very day.

In the kitchen, the two men—one old and one young, and both

set to die in a matter of hours—stand together, holding each other up. Even if they have never been able to speak, there is something shared between them, something that is the same in their bones, beyond words. This feeling of knowing his grandfather for maybe the first time keeps the young man sobbing until he hears the timer on the stove, which he set to let him know that the meat had thawed.

The beeping brings the young man back to reality—some lower level of reality, perhaps. He lifts his face from of his grandfather's shoulder, stands up straight, and nods to a face that looks much like his own, wiping away tears and snot with a paper towel. The grandfather says a final "atta boy," which for once is appropriate. Then, as if nothing happened, the old man grabs himself a fresh grape soda from the fridge, gives the young man a wink, and shuffles off down the hall.

1

Sometimes, when the young man has cried hard and is done crying, his lungs seem out of sync with the rest of his body. His inhalation is shaky and shallow, and his exhalation starts and stops. This is how he breathes now, as he sets the rest of the ingredients on the countertop beside the stove. Two glass jars of cherry tomatoes, painstakingly peeled and simmered down, make the base for the sauce. He dices and adds two Japanese eggplants, oblong and purplish black, along with some heads of garlic, small but with more flavor in a single clove than in the whole bulb of the unnaturally large store-bought kind. As he peels the garlic, he tries to get his body back into sync. He tries to breathe and focus on the moment as he crushes the cloves with the flat side of his father's favorite kitchen knife, into which is engraved *Badass Dad.*

While the sauce bubbles and simmers down to a mash and spits bits of red against the glass of the lid, the young man goes outside to get some fresh air.

He tries to ignore how close he is to dissociating so much that he won't have time to come back together before the end. He walks on the grass, feeling each strand of yellow-green between the spaces in his toes. The sun is still searing as the young man waters the garden for the second time today. The sun on the young man's clothes and skin feels like molten, pouring gold. When he comes back inside, the tile of the kitchen floor is cool and smooth and soothing. As he walks from the screen door to the stove, he leaves footprints of dirt and grass.

When the sound comes from the timer on the stovetop, he stirs the mix with a wooden spoon. He sets the timer again and waits for the slow bubble of the spices and slight sweetness of brown sugar to cut the bite of tomato acid. In three minutes, he will add the meat to the sauce. His breathing is almost back to normal; his lungs seem tight, but they are working. His family is moving beyond his sight around the house.

Outside, the dog is yapping skyward, and the sound is bouncing around inside the young man's skull. He has not thought of God or of trying to live a just life for some time now, and in the last ten minutes he has not thought of his girlfriend or of his sister. He has not thought of the end. He is simply trying to make a meal to feed those he loves, and in that, perhaps he is speaking to God louder than ever.

1

As the young man sets the table in the living room, the grandfather comes in from his room and sits down. He points at his grandson with the hand that isn't holding a soda can and says "Jesus Christ." The grandfather then sets the can on the table and starts speaking quickly, gesturing with both liver-spotted hands, repeating certain phrases slowly with overemphasized intonations, as if it's the speed of the language, not the language itself, that the young man is having a hard time with. There is a gap in the generations, a space between what the grandfather did to make a life for them here, away from the war and danger, and this young man, who can never quite know what his grandfather is saying or speak with him like anyone should be able to speak with his grandfather. Eventually, through his grandfather's gesturing, the young man is able to understand that he wants to hold hands. The young man takes his grandfather's hand, and eventually the mother comes into the room and translates that her father wants the family to say a prayer.

The young man's father saunters in as the rest of the family sits at the table holding hands. He has an unlit cigarette at the corner of his lips. His hair is slicked back. He is wearing a clean white t-shirt, which for him is fancy compared to his usual greyed tank top or tattered Carhartt long-sleeve. He smells of cologne, something the young man never would have guessed his father would own. The dark blue Levi's the father is wearing have been ironed. Between his tucked-in shirt and his jeans, the father wears a brown leather belt with a bronze buckle in the shape of an excavator. The father catches the young man eying his outfit, raises his eyebrows, and says, "Fresh to death." The mother and the son burst out laughing. The grandfather hushes everyone by clearing his throat. The father sits down and now the family is holding hands. The grandfather begins to recite a prayer that the young man and the father don't understand, but which the young man feels is the right, perfect thing to say. Midway through the recitation of the prayer, the doorbell rings.

It has been so long since any of the family has heard the doorbell that at first they don't recognize the sound. The father tells the family to stay put, motions for everybody to get under the table, sets his unlit cigarette on the table, and takes his buck knife off of his belt. He creeps toward the door. Cautiously, he looks through the peephole. He gasps and drops the knife, which sticks in the floor less than an inch away from his bare foot. He tears the door open and lets out a soft sound like the young man has never heard anything else make, somewhere between a gag and a cry.

The young man and his mother rush forward as the sister steps through the open front door, carrying a chrome suitcase and a dead fern in a terracotta pot. Her hair shows some grey strands and is cut into a messy bob that hangs over the tops of her eyes. She has a dark purple black eye and a healing split lip. She is wearing dirty Converse shoes, ripped blue jeans, and her evidently pregnant belly protrudes from beneath a dark green sweater the young man is pretty sure used to be their father's. In an overdramatic voice, she says, "Honeys, I'm home!" then collapses into her father's arms. As she falls, her grip loosens on the pot and it shatters, scattering soil, feathery wilted leaves, roots, and sharp orange clay triangles across the living room floor.

The father and the son half carry, half drag the young woman to the couch. The young man brings her a blanket, and the mother unlaces her daughter's shoes. The grandfather helps the father collect the pieces of the broken pot and sweep up the soil as the young woman regains her senses. She mumbles that the light through the living room windows is too bright. The young man closes the blinds, and the room turns a red-brown, soft dark like when you hold your hand up to block the sun but can still see the light through your skin. In this dirty rose glow, everybody in the family wants to ask the young woman where she has been, but her appearance is so dire and daunting that, instead, no one says anything and the young man silently embraces his sister.

The young man smells the faint musk of his sister's pear perfume and feels some solace in the fact that she still smells like herself. Her father follows and hugs his children, then the mother after that, and finally the grandfather wraps his arms around the four bodies on the couch. They sit like this until the young woman says she can't breathe. The family backs up from the couch. The grandfather brings a fresh can of grape soda over and offers it to his granddaughter. She sits up, weakly smiling, sips from the can, and asks, "What's for dinner?"

1

The young woman tells her family that she wants to eat dinner like nothing is wrong, that she hasn't come all this way with a bun in the oven and hell all around to be fawned over and made to feel like things are all weird. So the family gathers around the table, and the young man sets a place in front of the chair that has for so long sat empty.

The young man's main goal with the bolognese was to make it so the family would not be able to taste the elk meat, because they are all sick of it. The mix of cayenne and cherry tomatoes and a couple pinches of brown sugar made a hearty, spicy, sweet flavor which drowns out the gamey chewiness of the chunks of elk. The grandfather nods after tasting his first spoonful and doesn't water down each bite with grape soda like he does with most everything else, which the young man takes as a good sign. The mother nods too, trying to smile despite a full mouth. The sister gives her brother a thumbs up as some red sauce drips down the side of her mouth and onto her shirt, leaving a red stain which causes the sister to curse.

The father classifies this bolognese as *mighty fine slop*, which from him is high praise. The father has a system of dividing foods into *slops* and *glops* and other things that rhyme with those two words. For example, he calls oatmeal *glop* because, as he says, *it mostly sticks together*, whereas the young man's bolognese is more of a *slop*: *it ain't all one thing*. The first time his girlfriend ate with him and his parents, his father explained this system. The example he used was the blue cheese salad dressing she was eating, which was, in his system, *plop* because of the sound it made when you dumped it onto the plate. The young man was worried she was going to break up with him after that meal, but she only laughed.

Despite the intensity of the sister's return and the weight of what is coming in just a few hours, everybody seems to enjoy themselves. After the first few bites, the mother jumps up with an "Oh!" and runs down the hallway, slipping slightly on the hardwood in her mismatched socks. She comes back less than a minute later holding two bottles of wine. The bottles look old and the labels are fancy, swirled with gold lettering. She explains she was given the bottles by her publisher after the release of *Shtetl 51* in paperback and has kept them in the closet, imagining she'd never have an occasion to drink such expensive wine, but tonight is something none of them would have ever imagined and is the perfect and final occasion for anything. As his wife speaks, the father opens the first bottle with the multitool-knife he keeps on his belt beside his buck knife. The mother says to let it breathe for a few minutes, but none of the family waits, and as they pour the wine, the father raises his glass and says, "Here's to the prodigal daughter!" The mother raises her glass, and after she communicates to her father what is being said, he raises his glass. Once everybody has clinked and made eye contact and drunk long sips, the mother says that while she understands the sentiment her husband was trying to convey with the toast, she would be remiss if she didn't explain that the word *prodigal* doesn't actually mean what everybody thinks it means: "There's the story of the prodigal son in the Christian Bible, from which the phrase was adopted into common usage—but the son isn't prodigal because he returns. Prodigal means wasteful. The son returned because he ran out of money… So, well… She isn't really a prodigal daughter. It's kind of fascinating how prodigal son or prodigal daughter has come to mean one who wandered…." Here she trails off, everybody staring blankly at her. It's silent for a moment before the father gives his wife a big kiss on the mouth and says, "Gonna miss that brain of yours."

As the family eats their last meal, things feel as they haven't in years, or perhaps never did, everyone eating and laughing and drinking and whole. The sun outside is getting low, and it's getting hard to see, so they light some white and blue striped candles pulled from the drawer where they keep the menorah. The flickering of the flames makes the room seem to move and the faces appear long and ancient.

1

After dinner, the father goes outside with the grandfather to smoke and watch the sunset. The dotted yellow moths that come out after the sun has sunk circle and sizzle around the bulb above the door leading into the kitchen. The young man knows what his father and grandfather are going to do, because for many nights this month he has joined them, not smoking but pensive beside them. His mother takes a shower, during which her off-key singing can be heard around the house.

Everybody wants to be with the young woman, but she says that she's been waiting to wash the dishes with her brother for a long time. The young man says that he's happy to do every dish if she'll just sit next to him and talk. To this, she says she isn't going to use the end of the world as an excuse not to do her chores. The young man acquiesces and pulls up a stool and sits beside his sister as she takes her shift at the sink first. As she turns on the water, the kitchen is gilded by the light of the last sunset spilling across the sky, but neither of the siblings watches it.

The young woman wears yellow rubber gloves that go almost to her elbows because she has always hated the feeling of scraps of other people's food on her hands. Once, when she worked as a dishwasher during her first semester of college, she swore to never wash dishes ungloved again, covered, as she put it, in other people's half-eaten schmutz. Now, her yellow gloves squeak on the ceramic and steel, and because of her big belly, she has to lean over and stretch her arms to their full length to reach the faucet.

At first, despite all that they so need to say to one another, the two siblings don't speak. They simply enjoy being there together, existing with mere inches between them instead of the thousands of miles which have been the norm for nearly a decade. However, when the young man takes over at the sink and his sister sits on the stool where he had been, she breaks the silence. "Thanks for not asking how exactly I got pregnant." The young man starts to respond but decides not to when he sees his sister's eyes, glazed and pointed toward the ceiling in a failing attempt to keep herself from crying. Her hands are folded on her belly, the muscles in her throat trembling. She begins to speak again, and he continues to clean as she speaks because he fears she might stop talking if he gives her his full attention.

"After I broke up with Samantha—or she broke up with me—it was hard… But did you even know we broke up?"

"I don't even know anything about Samantha. I mean, I never knew there was a Samantha at all."

"Oh. Right."

And now they are quiet again, feeling the separation the years of silence have created. Their shadows are long and spread across the cabinets. Through the windows, the young man sees red clouds like wine stains on the sky. His sister says she was with Samantha for about a year, but it felt like they were going to be together forever, and after it was over she had no idea what to do. The young man nods and says he knows what she means. An image of his girlfriend's face flashes before his eyes. For a moment, he can do nothing and think of nothing but how her eyes shone when she looked at him.

"Well, it was hard. For a long time I didn't want anything, and I thought I'd never want anything again. But then a day came when I knew I wanted a child. I knew I wanted a child like I'd never known anything else, and I wanted it like I'd never wanted anything else. It wasn't easy, not a goddamn thing about it's been easy, but… Well, I found a way. As you can see."

"Is it a boy or girl?

"I wanted that to be a surprise. But I guess we'll never know, will we?"

The light shining through the windows is deep red, nearing purple. She says her baby feels like a girl, and she even had a list of names on her phone but deleted it after the Announcement. The young man says he likes simple names, and his sister says she likes those too. She describes how she was thinking of the name Sibyl, after their great grandmother.

Silence again, cut only by the clank of dishes on metal and the gurgle of soap and water down the drain. Eventually, the young man puts his hand on his sister's belly, which is wet from the dishes, and it leaves a print on her shirt when he takes it away. "Hello, Sibyl, nice to meet you. What a pretty name you have. You have a hell of a mom and an even better uncle who'd have given you anything you wanted."After the young man says this, he and his sister look away from each other. He glances into the sink. She looks out the window at the thin sepia of twilight, before the real darkness comes. The young man finishes washing the dishes in thick quiet. His throat has that tingle from not crying when he should have. He finishes the last plate, squeezes the water out of the sponge, stacks the plate in the plastic strainer at the end of the sink, then washes the bits of food and grey soap bubbles off his soggy fingers and palms.

The sister stands up from the stool beside him, walks over to the fridge, and stares at the pictures hung by magnets on its door, most of which are of the family without her. The young man turns off the water and comes to stand beside her. He asks, "Are you okay?" She says, "Of course not. Are you?" He responds, "Not really."

Stuck to the front of the refrigerator are a bunch of word magnets. Their father bought them for their mother for Hanukkah a couple years ago. They were the Yiddish word pack, which included classic words like *schlep*, *spiel*, and *shpilkes* in twelve-point Times New Roman. The same year their father got their mother the magnets, due to some miscommunication, the young man also got her a pack of magnetic words. He wanted to get her the Yiddish pack, as he had seen it at a friend's house and thought his mother would think it was funny, but his father had bought the last set. All they had left at the store was the poetry pack, including words like *opaque*, *essence*, and *liminal*. So he bought that one, which had been combined with the Yiddish words on the fridge.

The siblings now stand looking at the black letters on the pebbled white.

The dishes drip in the rack, and the droplets run down the plastic into the sink, making a sound like soft rain on a metal roof. Outside, the light is going away. The siblings start moving words into sentences. The sister comes up with the phrase, *Eat schmaltz and have a good time.* The young man says that if there were time and things were the way they used to be, they could have gotten matching tattoos of that phrase. The young woman laughs, but the young man is not sure if the laugh is in defeat or good humor. He then writes, *I schlepped my toches and my broken heart home.* They agree this is what they have both done, coming back to this place that is lonely and messy and hopeless and home.

The young woman reaches into a drawer by the sink, takes out a clean rag, grabs a still-damp plate from the rack, and wipes it dry with an expert swirl of cloth. She clears her throat as her brother stands aimless in front of the fridge. She hands him a dry plate and he takes it and puts it in its place in the cabinet. This continues until the dish rack is empty and they are giggling about some stupid memory from what seems like another life. And when they are done with the dishes, the young woman joins her father and her grandfather on the patio in the growing dark. The young man goes to his room to read the last page of his journal.

2

The last of the sun is gone, and with it went the future, for tomorrow comes the end. Even when there was a future, before the Announcement, it was nothing more than dreams or visions or plans of moving to some apartment in a subdivided house, in which maybe there's a dog you got from the pound, and maybe that dog has a crooked tail. Maybe the future's always been imagined snippets of a life which, at best, only *might* be lived, merely a fantasy of having the dog sit beside you while you're eating dinner or snoring softly as it sleeps between you and your lover. The thing about the future is that most of the time it never happens. The future's only ever been mirage and grand plans. Sometimes the future was nothing more than the smile on someone's face when you asked them to move in with you. Sometimes the future was the smile on your own face when this person said she'd love to. The future could even be the moment after you agreed to move in together, when you both started looking online for apartments with leases allowing pets. Maybe the future wasn't much at all, but just knowing there was one, that there was something to work toward, to wake up to, that was worth something.

If the future's only a gleam, the past is what we've had to hold onto: the solid, the scars, those long days that made us who we are. The past has marked us, named us, given us secrets to tell or not tell, filled our closets with clothes, most of which we'll never wear, filled our photo albums with scenes of us in places we'll now never go to or see again, standing beside people that are long gone or, at best, soon will be. But the past has always been just that: passed. And so often, I've found myself with nothing but the present moment to take in and find real. And today, without much of any future left and a past that seems to stretch on forever, it seems more important than before to not let the present slip away. But now too, this moment, this present, cast in a milky glow, feels both too short and infinite. But no matter the speed of time, the dark that is coming in just one day will spread like a tanker spill in the sea. It will spread until there is nothing left that it hasn't covered in its black.

1

The family gathers in the living room, everyone barefoot but for the grandfather in his slippers. They stand around the kitchen table not really knowing what to say or do, waiting for a ritual or a sign, until the mother blurts, "Well, it's been nice to know you all!" and begins sobbing. She does not say, *See you tomorrow* or *See you in the morning* as she might have done any other night. She does not speak in the future tense, for there is no longer such a thing.

Over the sound of the sobbing and the throbbing tension in his ears, the young man can hear the sound of his grandfather noshing almonds. The room smells like cigarettes on breath and dry summer night air. The family stands in a circle again, like they did by the fire before dinner, but this time they are not praying or setting anything aflame. They are simply together in the bulb-lit night. The young man is holding his mother's right hand with his left and his father's left hand with his right. His mother's hand is smaller than the young man's and cold to the touch. Her fingers are skinny and her nails are painted oxblood. This is a color he knows her to wear only on dates with her husband or other special occasions, like when she was on a panel at a conference or giving a reading. The young man supposes that his mother considers today a special occasion and that, yes, today is something special in the way a funeral is special. The young man looks across the circle and sees that his sister's nails are also painted, and on the air he again detects her pear fragrance. In fact, both the women are wearing this perfume, a tradition carried down through who knows how many generations, until the end.

The young man's father's hands have calluses on the inside of every knuckle and at the ridge between his fingers and his palm from tools and the bench press in the garage next to the freezers.

The young man can feel a line of scar tissue on the finger his father cut off the day he met his wife, a line of white like a promise ring engraved in skin. The father's hands are slightly shaking and sweaty, and the young man realizes another thing he inherited from his father.

The family stands for many minutes crying. Behind them, the spaces between the frames of the windows show mostly black. Then the circle breaks up as spontaneously as it formed. They find themselves around the TV, and soon his mother has put on the home videos. They watch the whole of their recorded lives: the siblings building a snowman in the front yard, the young man's first day of kindergarten, a school play the young woman performed in. The last thing they watch is the mother and father's wedding. In it, they see the grandfather looking young and dark-haired, still in his paper boy cap, walking his daughter down the aisle. And for a few minutes, it is perfect there on the couch. Nothing is evil or dying or dead. They all yell *mazel tov* with the breaking of the glass and again as the younger versions of the mother and the father are lifted up in chairs and carried offscreen.

1

We sit now in the garden, between the flowers and the fruit and the thin white moths, which flutter so softly they make no sound at all. After finishing our home videos, I took my notebook from my room and we all went outside. Zayde is chewing almonds pulled from his pocket and looking up at the sky, sipping on his final grape soda. Dad is leaning back against the fence beside the unripe eggplants with his arm around Mom. They're sharing a cigarette and smiling. My sister is behind me. We're sitting back-to-back, holding each other up. Our breath is now in sync, and I can feel a faint third heartbeat coming through my sister's body into mine.

Thousands of crickets hum around us in the night, a final buzzing chorus. There's another sound too: the constant racket of the end of days. Louder than ever, the dog down the street is doing its best version of a scream. The squeak at the end of each bark pierces the blackness, the insect song, my family's ears, and our composure. It's at the end of every one of that dog's breaths when I feel real fear, in the thin space between barks.

The air is cooler than it was in the house and smells faintly sweet from the night-blooming tobacco jasmine my girlfriend planted. Between two stems poking up out of the soft soil, topped with bright white petals, I see a sunflower sprout. The moon is a splinter in an atlas of black, and my family is all together. There is still a scent of fire from before, a white patch on the grass from where my dad sprayed the ground with the fire extinguisher, and a black circle from where the trash can sat. These are the remnants of all we have done.

Since the Announcement, there has been a constant rush of sound: an unbroken clang of far-off gunfire, car alarms, distant yelling—once, the boom of an airplane coming down a couple miles from here—and of course, the dog down the street. But now, for the first time in a month, all is muted, like even the world is holding its breath. The dog is no longer howling. Instead, it's making the audible form of a ghost, a low moan waning to complete stillness.

The wind has picked up, and in it I can see some of the unburnt sticky notes being blown out of the pine box where I kept them. One just landed on my leg, and I see on it her looped ballpoint scribbles, a final message from my girlfriend, a last bit of love to get me through: *"I've found that there is always some beauty left—in nature, sunshine, freedom, in yourself." –Anne Frank*

And now, someone far away is setting off fireworks. They shine for a second in the sky, like a flower cast in flame, before trickling down across the night.

ACKNOWLEDGMENTS

Thank you to Michelle Naka Pierce, who helped shape this from a mess of ideas for a thesis into a story.

Thank you to Mark Schwartzman, who read this so long ago and has never stopped asking when it was going to come out.

To the love of my life, to my family, to the few friends who get it, you hold me up and keep me together.

To the musicians who made the songs that form the backbone of this book. May your music carry us through this world and all the others.

Finally, thank you to Luke Hankins and Jonathan Geltner and the rest of the staff at Orison Books. Before the two years we have spent on this book together, I didn't understand how collaborative and intimate the process of editing a work of fiction could be. Thank you for your attention and love and care, and ultimately for believing in this little story enough to help foster it into the world. I have never worked so hard and long on a piece of writing in my life, and all this would not have happened without your acceptance of and hands-on work with this manuscript. This is ours.

ABOUT THE AUTHOR

Alexander Shalom Joseph is the author of the short story collection *American Wasteland*, the prose poetry collections *Broken Light in a Burning Wood* and *Our Mother, The Mountain*, and the poetry chapbook *Buttons and Bones*. He works as a carpenter and lives in a cabin in Colorado.

ABOUT ORISON BOOKS

Orison Books is a 501(c)3 non-profit literary press focused on the life of the spirit from a broad and inclusive range of perspectives. We seek to publish books of exceptional poetry, fiction, and non-fiction from perspectives spanning the spectrum of spiritual and religious thought, ethnicity, gender identity, and sexual orientation.

As a non-profit literary press, Orison Books depends on the support of donors. To find out more about our mission and our books, or to make a donation, please visit www.orisonbooks.com.

Orison Books is grateful to Richard Chess
for his financial support of this title.

For information about supporting upcoming Orison Books titles, please visit www.orisonbooks.com/support-us.